Every Time
I Think of You

JIM PROVENZANO

ACKNOWLEDGMENTS

Thanks to Adam Barrett, Jeff Ford and
John Harry Bonck for their early enthusiastic reads;
to Peter Fogel and Eric Himan for music assistance;
but especially to Stephen LeBlanc for advice
and support beyond the call of duty.

for Ed Gallagher

"In nature, nothing is perfect and everything is perfect. Trees can be contorted, bent in weird ways, and they're still beautiful."

– Alice Walker

Chapter 1
Winter, 1978

The open field outside my bedroom window beckoned and the woods beyond it promised another small adventure, the most unusual having nothing to do with wild animals or trees, but with a boy standing nearly naked in the snow.

On impulse and with a sense of restlessness, I snuck into the hallway and pulled a parka and gloves over a favorite worn T-shirt and sweatshirt. I left quietly to avoid providing a reason for my exit. "I'm going for a walk" might have seemed suspicious to other parents. As a mediocre distance runner who'd spent most of his free time in solitude, such jaunts were common. Besides, our days together over the holiday break had become a bit stifling.

My bedroom adjoined my parents' and my libido had years before outgrown the confines of our small one-level house. Were practicality the explanation for my spontaneous hike, I could have sung my purpose that afternoon, 'Wanking in a Winter Wonderland.'

Were I prescient, I might have said, "I'm off to meet my destiny, my other."

Midway across the field, I cautiously glanced back. Our neighbors' homes sat brightly in a row under sunshine bouncing off the field of snow. The back yards all faced the open field left undeveloped by the mandate of some deceased town elder with a penchant for kite-flying.

That afternoon there were no kites in the sky, merely a blank slate of blue. The sun, stark and silvery above, had begun to melt the nearly blinding expanse of iced snow that crunched under my footsteps. The ensuing shivers faded as my body warmed from the brisk walk.

I approached the strip of trees dividing Forrestville, the wealthy community of Greensburg town fathers and their families, from our mere middle class block of Pennsylvania homes.

Although I was probably being watched from the kitchen window by my mother, I felt I'd made a successful exit. My frequent off-season jogs and walks to the field, the adjoining woods, and eventually long runs to the countryside and mountain ranges a few miles away, proved my fascination for nature. In warmer seasons, my determination to pack a sleeping bag and spend a few nights in the woods left my generally supportive parents perplexed.

What probably would have shocked them, and the future college instructors, was the deeper motivation for my arborous interests. Our ranch house with its thin walls made the outdoors a much better option for what most other boys enjoyed in their bedrooms. I had developed a stronger sexual relationship with trees and plants than with any person.

Entering the edge of the small woods, I felt warmer and secure. I'd rarely encountered other people in that small expanse of trees and its charming creek, which is why I'd long considered it my own private refuge.

A thick blanket of snow lay at my feet, sleeves of it bending the limbs of shrubs. Bluish whites contrasted the dark limbs of the evergreen branches above.

Further in, the snow under the tall evergreens was softer, quieting my footsteps as I encountered something unexpected; a pair of grey sweatpants and a green parka hanging on a tree limb.

Then I saw him.

While leaning against an evergreen trunk, the pumping motion of one arm, his flexed buttocks and thrust hips revealed from behind what he was doing.

He turned to see me as I stood between him and his clothes, and thereby his escape, accentuating the hunter-meets-deer moment that was our first encounter.

Despite his pale skin, I saw how colorful he was. Most prominent was the red flush on his cheeks, fore and aft, the various tans and light browns of his backside, the green buffered light between his arms and along his almost stocky legs, and the nearly bluish-black of his hair, tousled and flattened, no doubt, from wearing the discarded ski cap at his feet.

At that sudden moment when he turned, me standing only a few feet away from him, I saw, after his initial surprise, the warmth in his eyes, which, on first sight appeared dark like onyx stones, almost black.

Unable to cover himself, he merely halted his strokes and looked at me, at first stunned. Despite having never met me, he welcomed me with a smile, as if expecting my arrival. Wearing only a pair of gloves and boots, the steam of his body heat rose from his groin and the arrested friction of his hands.

So many explanatory phrases reeled through my mind. *No,* I wanted to say, *don't stop. What a brilliant idea, bringing sweatpants that come off around your boots. Leather gloves work best, don't you think? Isn't it surprising how warm it is in winter under these evergreens? This is a great spot, but if you want to be truly daring, try the top of the nearby hill on a moonlit night.*

Stuffing my glasses in a pocket, shucking off my T-shirt, sweatshirt and parka as one, ripping my jeans down to my thighs, I clumsily approached and wrapped his smaller body in a shocked but welcome embrace. Our prolonged wet kiss didn't end until he'd clutched both our dicks to near completion. In a moment of inspiration, he tugged me by my erection closer to the tree, where we both spewed onto its trunk.

Quivering, knees buckling, our misty breath escaping with gasps and surprised chuckles, one thought remained at the forefront of my mind.

That thought was, *Where the hell have you been all these years?*

Chapter 2

We pulled apart, swaying, mutually dazed.

He hastily dressed and started ambling downhill and toward the row of back yards on the other side of the woods. As I fought to slip my clothes back on with much more difficulty than my abrupt disrobing, he had already walked yards away from me. I fumbled for my glasses, dropped them in the snow, retrieved and wiped them. Through the moist droplets on the lenses, I saw him standing a few yards from me, waiting.

Fully expecting that our encounter was the end of it, that he had regained his senses in a moment of regret, I was prepared to spend every successive afternoon of my winter break returning to that spot like some sort of lone creature pining for its lost mate.

But he simply cocked his head for me to follow, as if accompanying him were a matter of course.

The route into Forrestville had several paths, none of which I'd ever dared to take beyond the woods. Years before, I'd been in the neighborhood annually, one of many costumed children dropped off in cars by our parents on Halloween. The rich folks always gave away the best candy.

His steady pace, and a few footprints in the opposite direction, made it apparent that he knew the way. Was it his scent I'd unconsciously been sniffing all these years? Was he the real reason this little acreage held such interest for me?

I felt more like a trespasser than ever, sidling along a path between two large homes and out onto the street. But no one materialized to scold us or query our presence. Our footsteps broke fresh snow through yards, until we were upon shoveled and salted curving asphalt.

Had we been lovers of the opposite sex, this would have been the beginning of a class division romance of operatic proportions. As we were two horny seventeen-year-old boys, our encounter was a mere conspiracy.

"You live here?" I asked as we approached the largest mansion on the block, an imposing red brick Tudor house with a huge porch, a three-car garage, and a coned tower at one corner of the roof. I remembered being daunted by it on my childhood Halloween visits.

"Usually," he replied.

"What's up top?" I asked.

"Just part of the attic," he said. "Why?"

"I dunno. I think that pointy roof–"

"The turret?"

"Yeah. It's what made the older kids think..."

"What?"

I hesitated. In the few post-virginal minutes I'd spent with this handsome guy, he appeared to me a vision of lustful perfection, but might as quickly disappear from my life if I insulted his home.

But out it came. "They used to call your house Collinwood."

"Oh, jeez," he snorted. "From *Dark Shadows*?"

"Yeah."

"You townies. You're a hoot. Come on."

Despite its imposing presence, the interior of the house was warmly colored, full of inviting furniture, paintings and at least two fireplaces. The oversized living and dining rooms managed to maintain a cozy feel.

"Sorry, no ghosts," he grinned as he led me around in socked feet after we'd removed our boots in the foyer. An enormous Christmas tree stood fully decorated yet unlit in the expansive living room. He led me into an equally large kitchen.

Our smirking silence gave his family's housekeeper reason to offer me a few suspicious glances as she prepared hot chocolate and cookies, leftovers from what must have been a busy holiday season.

"Who's your new friend, Everett?" she inquired, as she stirred a small pot. It seemed she knew to have it prepared after her ward's outdoor trek.

A lesser version of that initial brief dark-eyed panic flashed on his face again as he rubbed his hands for warmth. He stared at me, realizing silently that we hadn't even bothered to share each other's names.

"Reid. Reid Conniff," I said, nodding curtly, as if I were some sort of servant. I had no idea how to behave. For the first few moments I mistakenly thought this portly woman was his mother.

"Helen's been taking care of us for, how many years, old girl?"

"Old girl?" She mocked him with a hint of amusement.

I sensed a mutual history of shared entertainments, secrets and dirty laundry, literal and figurative.

"Mom's often away," Everett said as he led me to sit at a table with him. "My sister moved out a few years ago. So, it's just us more often, eh... old girl?"

Everett's deliberate omission of mentioning a father led me to believe that divorce was the most probable unspoken explanation. Although I had no knowledge of his normal behavior —our woods encounter couldn't be regarded as an unbiased litmus test— I felt that Everett was performing for me with an air of casual ease that wasn't normally the case in such a household.

As she served us mugs of hot chocolate, Helen's vague inquiries about our sudden friendship were met with the most involved lie I'd ever heard. My own family life never included fanciful tales or any kind of scandal. I was unlearned in the art of the elaborate fib.

Everett breezily unspooled a convoluted plot about a hiking group organized by some schoolmate's local cousin and a sign-up sheet at the local library. As his tale continued, after his simple knee nudge under the table, I nodded agreement.

Helen, either satisfied or bored, said, "Just so long as you're not up to anything."

"Up?" Everett quipped, nudging me again. I took the reference to be sexual, and blushed. "Helen's tried to spank me, but she could never catch me. Here, these are the best."

He pushed forward a plate of cookies in the shape of Christmas trees with green glaze and sprinkled decorations.

"Trees, with icing."

Getting the inside reference to our amorous encounter, I nearly coughed up hot chocolate. Everett took another cookie, dipped it in his mug and ate heartily, his eyes on mine. "Reid," he whispered, as if savoring the sound of my name.

"He's misbehaved more often than not," she scolded.

"Really?" I said. Neither replied. Everett merely smiled and slurped from his mug.

"Thanks!" Everett saluted, nodding toward me to leave with him. I popped the last branch of a tree cookie in my mouth and offered a mumbled, "Thank you."

As if to offer me a sort of warning, Helen said to him, while looking at me, "What will you get up to this time?"

What we got up to over the next several months was a blossoming of my new life, my first attempt at knowing another boy by his gestures, his sound, his taste. I would dare to dive headfirst into another world of clumsy, passionate and impulsive acts.

I would borrow my mother's car to visit Everett's rebellious sister in Pittsburgh. I would secretively drive him into the poorer section of that city where, hooded like a gang member, he would purchase marijuana. I would commit several minor crimes in the service of our almost unstoppable appetite for having sex in unusual places. I would collude with Everett to drive his mother to the point of hysteria. I would nearly ruin my chances for a college scholarship by staying up into the early morning hours with Everett the night before a placement exam. I would connive and conspire, break and enter.

I would learn the varying temperature of erratic desire, the caloric output of longing, and the previously undefined and eventually unbearable weight of first love.

Chapter 3

Accepting Everett's invitation to see his bedroom, my consent was irrelevant as he bounded up the two-tiered staircase of his family's mansion. As I followed, I became distracted, not so much by the house itself, but the collective history displayed on its walls.

Leading up the stairs, a series of mostly chronological images began with some sepia portraits of men with old-fashioned mustaches and dark suits, and women in laced gowns with doll-like infants on their laps. More recent family photos of his parents' wedding, baby pictures and formal family portraits included Everett as a toddler, then a young boy, and more recently, his smiling face in a private school jacket and tie. A girl, then a young woman whom I assumed was his sister, projected a carefree disposition. Images of his father, who shared Everett's dark hair and good looks, were paired with photos of his mother. Amid the changing hairstyles, a somewhat stern and determined look grew over time in her eyes. The last and most recent photos excluded his father altogether.

My perusal of the portraits was interrupted. "Come on," Everett called from the top of the stairs.

Due to his frequent absence at private school, his room looked more like a boy museum, cluttered up by his recent return visit, as if an indigent had snuck into an archive and taken up lodging. Family photos, framed clippings of sports articles with a team photo, and a school pennant, seemed almost cliché. The only modern element was a poster from the Styx album *Grand Illusion*, which displayed a surreal image of a female face inside the silhouette of a rider on a horse, standing in between some intricate tree trunks.

Everett casually dropped his damp sweatpants on the floor. Helen had castigated him for not immediately changing when we'd entered the house; he'd ignored the command. I prepared myself for, and pretty much expected, another embrace.

Instead, Everett, completely naked, held out his hands like a comedian closing his show in a sort of "Ta da!" moment, then continued getting dressed before I could consider applauding.

I turned away from the sight of his beautiful body to look over his shelf of trophies. I removed my glasses (I'm nearsighted; it's distances that appear blurry) to see that Lacrosse, Debate Team, and Latin Club President were among his accomplishments, the last of which he proved by reciting something at my request; "*Vescere bracis meis.*"

"Which translates to?" I asked.

"Eat my shorts."

Because his school was private, and miles away, I'd never read of his deeds in our local newspaper. But it was his last name that struck me.

"Forrester? Are you *the* Forresters?"

"I'm not *the* Forrester. I'm *a* Forrester. My great-grandfather's the one you're thinking of."

Isaac Forrester, with some allegedly ill-obtained funds from investors of questionable repute, had bought up every stretch of land that is now the ritzy section of town and named it all after himself.

The only parts left undeveloped were the public park and the strip of trees separating Forrestville's residents from the surrounding neighborhoods.

I didn't feel the need to speak. The few other boys whose bedrooms I'd visited had made me feel obligated to fill the non-sexual awkwardness of budding friendship with chatter about anything and everything. These had been pimpled fellow science lab nerd acquaintances for whom I'd felt no desire, other than to corroborate homework notes.

Despite this, it being his bedroom (I would yet see his dormitory, a more primal and ripe environment, I hoped), I felt what Everett would later bluntly say of my own bedroom, "I wanna sneak in here and hump every surface."

As he finished changing into a sweatshirt with the name and emblem of Pinecrest Academy, I sat on a chair at his desk, secretively looking for some small memento to pilfer.

"We should go into Pittsburgh. I want you to meet my sister, Holly," Everett said with sudden enthusiasm.

"We could take the train," I suggested. "I've done that a few times. It's only, like, an hour."

Actually, I'd only done that a few times with my mom when I was a kid. We had gone shopping before Christmas while Dad was at work, before she got her own car. I remembered the trips as special adventures as we'd chosen gifts for Dad. I don't remember ever believing that Santa brought presents, but that they were shipped by rail. Even my own gifts were rarely surprises after the time I was eight. I'd begun making little lists of potential gifts, arranged by price and referring page numbers according to whichever catalogs we had in the house. Clearly, I had inherited my dad's accountancy skills.

Everett interrupted my thoughts with, "Don't you have a car?"

I resisted the urge to snap, "Don't you have a chauffeur?"

"I don't have a driver's license, see," Everett said. "Never got one." That would prove to be one of many lies Everett told me; inconsequential, all of them, compared to one great lie.

"Why do you want to visit your sister?" I asked, in an attempt to divert him from my uneasiness in asking to take a family car into Pittsburgh. "Why isn't she here?"

"Oh, she stopped by for Christmas, but she works. She was done with the 'holly jolly' jokes a long time ago. And well, you know, sitting around with the family gets tiresome after the big day."

I did know, but in a different way. My mother's brother and his wife ended up becoming the most fertile of pairings in our peasant lineage. After their fifth child, they bought a huge home in a suburban development outside of Scranton whose square footage probably matched Everett's home, but whose design and décor more resembled a Days Inn.

They became the default holiday host, since their assembled entourage didn't export well. We endured the four-hour trek across Pennsylvania on usually snowy roads. My father's parents were annually retrieved from a retirement village outside of Scranton. I disliked a few of my much younger cousins, for reasons that involved their habits of screeching, violent dares with toy weapons usually aimed at me, and their infrequent bouts of projectile mucous.

Understandably, my parents and I spent the remainder of our holiday recovering by reading books and generally enjoying a rather non-Christmasy Christmas.

"So, how about Saturday?" Everett pressed.

"To visit your sister."

"That's not the point, brainiac." Everett softly punched my shoulder. "We can be alone together; spend the night. Together."

"Oh."

It was Wednesday. The new year approached on Sunday, and a new semester would begin the next week. I'd just abruptly become a man, of sorts. I hadn't left the town border in months, aside from a Kansas concert at Three Rivers Stadium with a herd of the guys on the cross country team.

Everett beguiled me with his sudden anticipation. The fact that he was so quickly adhering me to his family, his life and his plans, was heartening and so unlike the post-coital rejection I'd expected.

That he employed a sort of bargaining chip only increased his charm. He, the scion of our town father, would owe me.

"Sure."

"Great! She works for the opera company. We can see a rehearsal, maybe."

While that opportunity had little appeal to me, the potential trip posed a problem. How was I to explain the request for my mother's aged Plymouth? I'd borrowed it for countless errands, done more for her with it, and never so much as scratched or dinged a fender. A few times, Dad had cautiously let me drive his newer Pontiac, but the majority of those trips had been local.

I enthusiastically shared with Everett the scheme that a visit to the Carnegie Museum of Natural History would suffice. I would have to check on their holiday hours, be sure of which exhibit we'd pretend to see, then perhaps actually stop by and purloin a brochure as evidence.

I would invent, and perhaps even create, an extra credit report needed for what I suddenly foresaw, and hoped for, as compensation for a spring semester full of delinquent exploits with Everett. I'd have to take notes to prove my research was well done. As a part-time stenographer for a small law firm, my mother often perused my homework notes for their efficiency. I wasn't getting a possible full scholarship without years of mildly persistent parental coaching.

As all these concocted plans ran through my head, I failed to notice that I was being casually seduced by my host.

Everett had turned on his stereo, preset with a small stack of LPs. Fleetwood Mac's *Rumors* began to play. He flopped down on his bed, bounced up once while scooting to one side, patted the other, coaxing me to join him like some newly trained pet.

Glancing down at the damp remnants of melted snow at my pants cuffs, I remembered that he did have a housekeeper, after all, and with an attempted gesture of élan, I plopped myself down beside him.

I didn't want to force myself on him again. But after a few minutes of the both of us simply staring at the ceiling, our legs and elbows touching, Stevie Nick's nasal voice warning that 'players only love you when they're playing,' I did.

Leaning up and over, I brought my lips to his, and with equal abruptness, Everett's face and mine collided. A chuckle, a lip wipe with tongues, and our mouths slurped together like sea anemones.

Everett slipped his finger between us to wipe away a liquid that I realized was dripping from his nose. Our bodies were literally melting after being outdoors.

Our embraces led to some awkward fumbling on my part. I instinctively understood Everett to be the more experienced. I understood sex, having read pretty much anything I could find in books. Two years earlier, I'd gotten a special library card at the local branch of Penn State given to high school honor students. From what I'd read, I knew what I was, and what men did with each other, in theory. In practice, I fumbled.

Our hands, much warmer now, and not gloved, grasped each other's erections while under the confines of undershorts, and in Everett's case, a fresh pair of sweat pants.

He being the host, and more nimbly fitted for undressing, Everett pried himself from me, rose up to kneeling, shucked down his sweatpants, his erection bouncing free. But as I grasped it like a handle, he scooted awkwardly off the bed, sweatpants at his knees in a comic waddle, softly locked his bedroom door, waddled back, and directed his cock at my face.

The next few minutes were an unrefined series of positions that failed to make my mouth accommodate his stubby girth and my lack of oral technique.

Sighing with mild disappointment, Everett pulled out of my mouth and seemed to decide that I could learn by example. He straddled over me and clamped his mouth around my dick. I hadn't a clue about relaxation or sexual response delaying techniques, nor, I suppose, should I have. His version done to me felt much more enthusiastic.

Everett shoved his mouth down further upon me, my moans of pleasure silenced by him stuffing himself atop my mouth, his legs shifting to either side of my head. After a few yanks of his sweatpants, finally, we fit together. This gave me an up-close view of his butt, which enticed me to explore that option. But before I could share more than a few playful rubs and finger-pokes, we were busy exploding.

The act of swallowing his bursts shocked me at first. Despite my attempt to move my hips away from his face, he was determined to do it to me. Besides, I would have otherwise left his bed splattered with evidence. Most important, he tasted pretty good, like glue, salt and sugar.

His appreciative gesture made me laugh with relief. Everett collapsed opposite me, then used his tongue to wipe his mouth. "Mmm. Cream of Reid."

We were partially clothed, arms wrapped around each other, half-sleeping in a tingling bliss, the stereo already on to another LP (Steely Dan) by the time Helen knocked on the door to announce that she had his laundry. Everett calmed me with a shouted, "Leave it outside, please," a cozy faux-yawn, and a sleepy smile, followed by a soft kiss.

I hastily dressed, then found my glasses, looked around for my boots before remembering they were downstairs in the doorway. The thought of facing his housekeeper, wondering if she would know or conjecture what had happened between us, worried me.

"So, stay for dinner?"

"Uh, no. Thanks."

"So, then. Saturday?" Everett was already preparing to escort me downstairs, as if he'd known that enduring dinner with his family, or whatever there was of his family, would be preposterous. I longed to walk back through those woods and stomp in the snow for joy, to lick my lips with what, or whom, I'd eaten. I wanted to avoid contact with other people, to savor this sacrament, my belated holiday gift.

As if sensing my apprehension at more introductions or staff encounters, Everett quietly led me down the stairs and through the momentarily empty kitchen.

"Come to think of it," he conjectured as I fumbled into my boots.

And then I stiffened inside, preparing for a rejection.

"I don't think I want to wait that long."

"Huh? I can't just take my mom's car. I have to … I can't use that B.S. you said about a library sign-up sheet. I have to–"

"Shh. I was trying to–" Everett looked me up and down like a coach whose rookie player left him slightly disappointed. "I'll come to visit you tonight. Helen's cooking leftovers anyway."

Perhaps it was the heat of being once again fully dressed in my parka, boots and all, but I melted again.

Yes, he would charm my parents. They, like me, would do their best, on the surface, to ignore the oddity of their bookish child having suddenly acquired the handsome son of the wealthiest family in our tiresome town as his friend.

That they were neither religious nor conservative assured a drama-free development as Stage Two of our friendship would be revealed. No, that would be the least of our problems.

Everett turned to the kitchen table, grabbed a paper plate of cellophane-covered tree cookies, handed them to me as a parting gift, turned his head both ways in a cartoonish sneaky gesture before planting a parting kiss on my cheek and whispered, as he ushered me out the door, "We're gonna be great together."

Chapter 4

When the phone rang, I was in the garage taking off my boots. Beside them were my muddy running shoes and a few pair of my parents' winter boots. I'd been chastised a few times to clean mine, but when faced with the logical explanation that they'd only become muddy or wet again, Mom always gave in.

I sat on a small pile of cardboard boxes, cartons of maple syrup, probably. My father, once a lowly accountant before I was born, had gradually been elevated to district manager of Best Rite, a company that bought regional foods wholesale and resold them to grocery stores and shops throughout the county.

Despite our ample supply of slightly dented cartons, cans and jars of preserves, cheeses and syrup, we refrained from excess consumption, mostly because of my mother's frequently stated distaste for what she called, "Germanic cuisine."

Mom sometimes served picture-perfect recipes from the old magazines she saved, all with a sense of humor about it. She'd even put up a few of her favorite culinary illustrations under magnets on the refrigerator. I suppose it inspired her. On special nights, hams appeared topped with pineapples and pink cherries, or roasts were adorned with amusingly trimmed potatoes. It wasn't until I'd dined at boyhood friends' homes that I realized such meals weren't a joke to other people.

I heard my mother pleasantly chatting on the phone for several minutes. I thought she was discussing some bit of gossip with one of our neighbors. Mom engaged in social activities with a few of the nearby wives, but maintained an air of remove. Although she never stated it outright, I felt that she found most of the women she'd met in Greensburg lacking in intellect.

She finally approached the door of my bedroom, where I'd just sat down. I'd been pretending to get a jump on next semester's reading, but was half-seriously wondering if I could find out the possible genetic side effects of orally ingesting the DNA of a loved one.

"Knock, knock," Mom chirped. Her dusty blond hair was tied in a ponytail. Her slim pants and post-holiday sweater gave her a youthful look.

"Your friend? Everett? On the phone." Her upraised emphasis noted a hint of curiosity.

"Were you ... talking with him that whole time?"

"Yes. He sounds like a very nice boy."

My over-reaction may have spurred her suspicion, since I pretty much leapt up, then adjusted to a false calm as I preceded her back to the kitchen phone, which hung on a wall next to a small memo pad.

"Hello?" I said.

"Look out your window in ten minutes."

"Hey, how's it going," I practically shouted, my phone voice clanging with insincerity. Everett had hung up. I suddenly pressed a finger down on the receiver and invented a short one-ended conversation filled with a few too many 'Okay's and 'Uh-huh's, then said goodbye to no one.

"So, your friend's coming over?" Mom said in an attempt at casual bemusement.

"Uh, yes?" Had he asked to be invited? Did she invite him?

Everett would be my first dinner guest in years, since seventh grade, when a boy named Ricky Chambliss thought wolfing down mashed potatoes and burping were common etiquette. Several of the guys from the cross-country team had visited one fall afternoon for a team party. For the most part, they ate and muttered inside jokes, then left as soon as the food was gone. For a skinny bunch, they could wolf down Mom's creatively arranged hot dogs almost as quickly as she served them.

I told myself that my general friendlessness had more to do with my studious nature, denying a mild fear that my slightly sarcastic parents and our contented life were a bit boring.

It wasn't that I was embarrassed by my small home and inconsequential life. I was more interested in being elsewhere with the few friends I'd had until then.

I just wondered how Everett had managed to charm my mom so quickly.

"I guess. Yeah," I stated vaguely.

"Will he be staying for dinner?"

"If that's okay?"

"Of course," Mom sauntered past me, perhaps inspired to put a little more whimsical pizzazz into whatever meal she would prepare.

"Who's coming over?" My father's voice carried from the living room over the low television tones of the evening news.

"Reid's new friend, Everett. Everett Forrester."

A pause, then, as expected, Dad asked, "*The* Forresters?"

I visibly rolled my eyes, a small performance for my mother, as if we were nonchalant about our guest, when in fact we were both a bit giddy for entirely different reasons.

"Yes, Dad. *The* Forresters."

"Well," was all I heard, as if he knew his consent or opinion were superfluous. Amid the confusion of my having to for almost the first time fake my emotional state in the presence of my parents, I'd forgotten our charmer's instruction. I retreated to my bedroom and realized its purpose.

From my window, in the middle of that snowy field, darkened from the fading dusk light, he emerged from that now precious strip of forest. I wiped my glasses, put them on, peered out and remained fixed on him as he approached, a lone dark figure whose form grew with each step. Seeing me in the window, he performed a little snow-kicking dance while balancing something in one hand, then headed toward me.

I remembered my previously unasked question, *Where the hell have you been all these years?* The answer, at least during holidays and summers, was apparently about three hundred paces due south.

From outside, my bedroom window was just above chest level. Impulsively, I opened it, shoved up the screen as well, leaned out like a suburban Juliet, and accepted a frozen welcome kiss from my beau.

"You have to invite me in through the door," he smirked, "like a vampire."

Chapter 5

To say that Everett's presence as our family's first dinner guest in months was impressive would be an understatement.

Everett charmed my mother by bringing a freshly baked pie, made by Helen, he explained in a polite manner that dodged the fact that his mother couldn't boil water. My mother rarely served desserts, not through any dietary restrictions, but mere disinterest. She treated the pie like a rare prize.

As I took Everett's parka, his green V-neck sweater with a tie and button-down shirt peeking out appeared more formal than I'd expected. Then I realized his clothes were everyday wear at his school. Still, my own flannel shirt and jeans seemed too casual by comparison.

My father was gradually bowled over as Everett, who had won trophies for the debate team (extemporaneous category), engaged him in discussions ranging from philosophy to national politics, all with a precocious maturity that I found a bit contrived.

After re-crafting the story of our initial meeting that he'd told his housekeeper, again minus the snowy woods and any reference to it, my parents seemed less suspicious of him.

Over a dinner that surprisingly featured fewer olives on toothpicks or side dishes with faces made of cornichons than I'd expected, the conversation revolved around my guest.

The questions my mother asked focused around Everett's family life. I felt almost jealous that his story was told for all of us, information he had yet to share with me.

"My family, as you know, has a long history with Forrestville."

"They *are* Forrestville," Dad added, a joke that fell flat.

"Yes, in a way," Everett acknowledged, immune to my father's comment. "My father left us a few years ago. My mom's busy with some charity work, League of Women Voters, that sort of thing."

"Oh." Mom perked up at the mention of any sort of political or feminist sensibility. Such women were rare in our town.

Everett affectionately told of his sister, Holly, the big city dweller, and his infrequent visits to see her. I sensed a game being played, as if the mention of Pittsburgh was a key he'd just inserted, and the lock was clicking open.

As I chewed my food, mostly in silence, I realized the purpose of Everett's affable behavior. He intended not only to assure them that my time with this new friend would be safe, but also informative, educational and even a bit of a status boost.

My parents were being played.

A flush of embarrassment overcame me as I found myself gazing at Everett as he spoke, smiled and nodded to me. His throat, sprinkled with the slightest of stubble, his strong chin and flat nose, made him appear mature beyond his years. His comportment confused me, as if I were having a secret affair with an adult. It didn't make my self-restraint any easier when, since we'd been seated next to each other, Everett had removed one of his loafers (which he'd worn on his walk under rubber galoshes) to graze his socked foot along my shin.

"What's so funny, son?" Dad asked.

"Oh, nothing," I blurted. Instead of shoving Everett's socked toes away, I spread my legs wide under the table, giving him more access.

I decided to take Everett's boldness a step further. While part of me wanted to bluntly state what should have been obvious, that we were more than friends, I could hardly say that we were dating. We had yet to seal the plan of what I'd hoped would be our first date. I tossed the dare back to our guest. "I was thinking of a story Everett told me the other day."

At that moment, I clumsily attempted his game, the art of the innocuous fib. "The one about lacrosse." I openly nudged him, saw the sly twinkle in his dark eyes, acknowledging that I was beginning to play along.

Of course Everett would have a lacrosse story. With a graceful wipe of his napkin, Everett told a succinct tale about one of his teammates hurling the ball into the stands and into the lap of the school dean's wife. It was innocuous, and our laughter was the perfect cue that dinner was concluded.

As we retreated into the living room, my mother stoically refusing bussing assistance, Everett made himself comfortable on our sofa, I at the other end, and my father in his usual recliner chair. I almost expected him to offer Everett a cigar and a snifter of brandy.

As a family, we generally eschewed the drone of the television, and instead listened to some of my father's jazz or classical LPs. Dad chose a Stan Getz album. Mom's preference ran toward older pop favorites; The Mammas and The Pappas, Doris Day, Dean Martin. Off to the side, my few rock albums filled the rack.

Everett, after dropping a few names like Coltrane and Gillespie, again doffed one loafer, tucked one leg under his other knee, and settled further back on the couch near me.

It took some reserve not to simply lay my head in his lap, I was that happy. My parents might have been initially miffed, surprised or even put off, more by any open display of affection than by it being between two boys, one of them their son. Learning by Everett's example, I realized that perhaps joy contained might have more longevity.

Dad asked Everett about his college plans, to which he replied, "Pre-Law, maybe, or Public Policy, with perhaps a minor in Classics. I thought of International Studies, but my French is a bit rusty. I'm still undecided."

"Well, isn't it great, not having homework for a while?" Dad added.

"Actually," Everett countered, "your brainiac son was telling me how much he's itching to see that new exhibit at the Carnegie Museum in Pittsburgh."

Did I reveal any surprise or embarrassment? Was I even by that night mastering the craft of social artifice?

"Are you sure it'll be open on New Year's Eve day?"

"Yes!" I chimed in, perhaps too quickly. I would have to call the museum to be sure.

"Well, why don't you boys take Anne's car?" My dad said. "I'll be home with my car in case she needs to go anywhere."

"We could take the train," I offered.

"No, it's fine."

Being handed the opportunity for what I'd hoped would be an entire day with Everett, my stomach performed a small flip-flop. No, it would be a day and night with Everett, preceded by a perfunctory trek to gaze at ancient plants under glass, and ending with a romantic night in his sister's most probably lavish guest room. This all whirled through my imagination until I felt a pang of shame at having witnessed my parents so easily become complete suckers.

Everett's conspiratorial wink told me it didn't matter. The sale had been made.

Having almost succeeded in mentioning with a casual air that I'd walk Everett home, "for part of the way," my mother warned me, "Don't go running at night. I don't want you tripping in some snow bank."

She knew I had a propensity for off-season jaunts rarely preceded by a proper warm-up, and sometimes without proper clothing or my glasses. I promised to keep myself to a pedestrian pace.

Our coats on, my parents properly thanked and bid goodnight by Everett, we were soon out in the field, half-heartedly attempting to retrace our footprints from the other direction. All the houses along our street had kitchen windows facing south toward the field. The buffered light afforded an eerie yet safe glow across the field, making night sledding a pastime for younger children.

Fortunately, no one was playing that night. Everett took his gloved hand in mine. Unsatisfied by our lack of direct contact, he rushed a quick peck to my lips.

"That was great," he marveled.

"You're quite the diplomat."

"You think they like me? Hey, are you being sarcastic?"

"Yes, they did. And I mean you're very charming. My parents don't easily take to new people. I think they're happy I finally have a friend who isn't a mouth-breather."

Everett broke away, trotting ahead, his arms spread out in a sort of off-kilter waltz.

"Have you ever gotten stoned?"

"Duh!" I blurted with a bit too much assertiveness.

I had smoked pot on three occasions, each of them while en route to rock concerts at Three Rivers Stadium with fellow teammates and a few older boys. Despite my quiet nature, I wasn't a complete stick in the mud.

"Good. When we get to the city, we can score some weed with one of her friends."

"What?"

"My sister."

"Your sister."

"Yup. Oh, don't worry. I'll pay."

"Um. Okay."

"We should just say we're sleeping over. My sis'll call your mom. She'll be cool."

"Cool, like a friend of a drug dealer, or cool like you?"

"What?" Everett whirled about, stopped, rushed to me. "I don't get to do this at school. There's no one like you. It's like…"

"Like a private school?"

"Yes. This–" He shoved himself close to me, forcing a kiss, another cold one. I was beginning to develop a preference for visible exhalations and frozen snot. As our lips parted, he kept his arms around me, cocking his head back to gaze at my face with a jaunty admiration. "I want to have adventures with you. I want more."

"Okay." I hesitated, but refrained from glancing around warily. In the middle of the field and the safety of its darkness, I embraced him again fully, kissed him open-mouthed, both of us humming with pleasure, satisfaction and anticipation.

"Besides," he added, as we finally pulled apart to merely hold gloved hands. "Stoned sex is so fuckin' amazing!"

He darted away, then turned back toward me in a playful tackle that led to us rolling around in the snow, which was fun until he shoved a handful of it down the back of my pants. As much as I suddenly adored him, laughing, I had to say goodnight and excuse myself, since I was almost literally freezing my ass off.

Chapter 6

I had hoped our drive to Pittsburgh would provide an opportunity for some lengthy intimate conversation that would bond us, and it did. I had also hoped we might even pull over at a rest stop and take advantage of some mythical erotic playground in the woods nearby. That distant possibility had hatched in my mind through some vague innate instinct, and the recent spate of public indecency arrests that had been documented in our local newspaper. It was probably for the better that nothing like that happened.

After a call from Everett's sister Holly about our accommodations, and the promise of an alcohol-free environment, my mother seemed relaxed about our overnight road trip.

My father expressed some doubts about potential "funny business," but nevertheless gave me twenty dollars for gas. My mother handed me another twenty, which I discretely palmed, "For food or whatever." I was also given a stern warning about not drinking, at least while driving. They knew I'd indulged a few times, but remained only mildly concerned, since I'd failed to return home from those few teenage parties completely drunk, and never while driving.

My journey began with picking Everett up at his home. I had hoped to ring the doorbell and be welcomed in like a reputable suitor, in a meager imitation of his previous dinner performance at our house three nights earlier.

Before I had even put the car into park, Everett came dashing out of the front door and down the driveway, wearing a parka with a small duffel bag over his shoulder. He tossed it onto the back seat as he hopped in, slammed the door, and impatiently drummed the dashboard, hooting, "Let's roll, my man!"

We instantly agreed to shift the meager car stereo away from my mother's preset stations of public radio and classical music to a few nearby rock stations. Everett's futile attempts to hone in on a distant university station that he said played jazz (it seemed he actually liked it) resulted in more static than saxophones.

My hints at physical affection, my hand on Everett's thigh, and my repeated longing glances toward him as I drove, were at first met with a calm acceptance. The purpose of the trip was being together, so why was he so aloof?

I knew quite well which directions to take to get to the highway and which probable exit to take once we approached the city; I-76 to I-376 west, or just I-376 west. My dad said it was more scenic, but my mom said he took the route to avoid the toll roads.

Busying himself with a map from the glove compartment, Everett insisted on playing the role of navigator.

I twice asked Everett to give me his sister's address.

"She's in Squirrel Hill. Don't worry. Just drive," he said with a steely calm. I was silenced in the matter.

After a few minutes of that silence, Everett must have realized I was upset. "Buh furs, wheeze gun don ton."

"What?"

"We's goin' downtown? Piss-barr-geeze!" he grinned.

I then understood. Many of the locals in Greensburg, but in particular people in parts of the entire state, had a certain twangy accent that we fortunately lacked. Even in his attempt to cheer me, Everett did it at someone else's expense. I shook my head, grinning nonetheless.

Was this what having a relationship would be like, backing down to keep the peace, enduring bad jokes? I had no such example from my parents. As long as I could remember, they had never argued. They did tell quite a few bad jokes, though.

The mood in the car eased as we began sharing stories of self-discovery, early crushes on other boys.

Then Everett stated with a kind of blunt pride, "So, I'm your first guy, right?"

I offered a bashful grin. "Yes."

"Have you dated girls?"

"Sort of." I'd asked a handful of girls out when formal dances required such ruses on a seasonal basis, but none of them more than twice.

"What about the guys on your team?"

"What? Oh, hell, no. They're … they're too much like me; loners, kind of. There is one guy, really popular, a pole vaulter. He lives near you, I think."

"Oh, really?"

"Yeah. Kevin Muir. Drove a bunch of us to a few rock concerts. You know him?"

He hesitated. "Oh, yeah. His dad owns the car dealership."

"Right."

"Yeah, I knew him when we were little. Bit of a jerk."

"Really? You think so?"

"All of us rich brats are jerks in one way or another." Seemingly determined to change topics, he said, "So, nobody on your team ever...?"

"Oh, no."

My cross country teammates were vaguely divided into two categories, stoners and nerds, with one lone devout Christian who thankfully limited his preaching to outside practices or tournaments. They never expressed doubts about my sexuality. I never got a hint of flirtation from any of them, possibly because I didn't offer it myself, and wouldn't have known how. None were close friends, and I was far from a star athlete, so they didn't seem to care what I did or didn't do.

But I wanted Everett to care. I wanted to care about him, and find a common ground that would settle my freshly unleashed affection toward him.

"What about you?" I asked. "You're more..."

"What? Slutty?" He fake-punched me.

"No, just experienced."

"There was an older guy at school. He graduated." I caught a faraway look in his eyes, wanted to ask more.

"Any, uh, 'townies'?"

"Ha. Perhaps. But you wouldn't want me telling other guys about you, would you?"

I shrugged agreement, but wasn't so sure. Something in me wanted to share this giddy feeling, but I knew it was too soon.

Everett shifted to telling tales of family conflicts and dramas, and the peer pressure and scholastic competition at his pricey school.

"If I don't keep a four-point-oh, if I don't get into a 'top-notch' school," his mother's term, he revealed, "like Carnegie Mellon, I'm sunk. I'd have to go to some state school —no offense— plus, it's bad enough that neither my sis or me are destined to marry or breed, so we're basically the end of the family tree, which disappoints them even more."

"The Forrester tree," I joked.

He barely smirked in reply. "Which is why," he scooted closer, turning on the charm, "I do so enjoy a little R and R with my new studly skinny dude."

"Hey, I'm not skinny."

He smiled, rubbing his hand on my thigh as he furled his eyebrows with a sort of Groucho Marx innuendo. "I bet you wanna pull over now, doncha?"

"I bet I do," I replied, slowing the car down, signaling as I pulled to the right lane in between the sparse weekend traffic. The roads were clear of snow, but coated in a crust of road salt.

Everett reached for the radio dial, turned down the volume, and suddenly blasted in a bright a cappella, "Anticipation! An-ti-ci-pay-yay-shun, is makin' you wait."

While the Carly Simon song was memorable, it still brought to my mind the ketchup commercial. Like the song, I waited.

For the rest of the drive, I let Everett tell stories that were less serious, laughed at his jokes, asked more questions, fascinated by him as I stole glances at his handsome face. While he continued acting relaxed, I would notice him fidgeting or repeatedly tapping his legs to the beat of the music. Perhaps he was as nervous as I was.

As we approached the city, after a half-serious argument over directions, Everett relented to my preference. Route 30 was the easy side way in, but for the big impact, I cut across one of the bridges, back around through Mount Washington, then drove through the Fort Pitt tunnel. He saw the reason for my determination. We cheered at the fantastic view of the skyline from the front with the three rivers' convergence into an actual point.

"We're almost there."

"Whoo-hoo!" he shouted.

"Sing another song."

"I don't have anything memorized."

"What, no choir trophies to go with all those others?" I taunted.

"We don't have a choir at my school."

"Well, pick something off the radio."

He raised the volume, searched back and forth, half-heartedly fumbling the lyrics to a few hits, until a mutual favorite's tinkling piano intro played, The Babys' "Every Time I Think of You."

Everett's singing was so open-throated, so honest, unlike his somewhat rehearsed demeanor with my parents. He turned the volume up high, coaxing me to sing the back-up vocals, albeit a few octaves lower, as he belted out each high note with fervor, occasionally marred by a cracked note, which only endeared him to me more.

"People say a love like ours, will surely pass..."

Hearing him so close to me, the pure mutual joy we shared, must have been what led me to realize I was falling in love with him.

"And every time I think of you..."

"Every time..."

"Every time I *think* of you..."

"Every single time..."

"It always turns out goo-ood!"

Our eyes met for brief moments mid-song. Somewhere in my heart, deep down in my gut, in that moment, in the middle of our hurtling drive through that tunnel, shedding my forgettable previous existence, I became determined for the first time in my small life – and not again, it would turn out, for a long time afterward – to learn how to have and to be a boyfriend.

Chapter 7

Holly's apartment was less than stately. My assumptions, based on her family's home and apparent wealth, had misled me. When we arrived, I at first mistook the looming Victorian as entirely hers. Snow lay thinly on lawns and roofs of other homes along the tree-lined block.

As Everett led me into the large foyer of the house, I realized my mistake. The front hallway had a row of half a dozen mailboxes inserted into a wall opposite the stairs. Along the hallway, what had been rooms in an expansive home had been divided into several apartments. Everett led me up the stairs and to one of several other doors that had numbers placed on each one.

It felt both odd and comforting to enter the home of someone I had yet to meet. A few casually placed French Impressionist posters shared wall space with a series of framed photographs of Paris street scenes and costume sketches which were presumably Holly's work. Plants sat on tables and a few standees by the large curtained windows. Late afternoon sun gave the room a bright warm feeling.

I heard the clink of Everett tossing his keys onto the kitchen table. His "Ah-ha," drew my attention through the doorway as he pulled a note from a magnet on the refrigerator.

"'Singing animals may keep me late,'" Everett read, slightly confused. "'Make yourselves at home.' Huh. I guess the opera she's working on has a zoo."

He turned to me, peeled off his coat, tossing it casually over one of the kitchen table's chairs. "So." That flirtatious leer again. "Let's get comfy."

With that, he was on me, wrapping me in his arms before I'd removed my coat or dropped my own duffel bag. His mouth tasted of the burgers and fries we'd eaten at a drive-through burger place along the highway. That didn't stop me from returning his kiss.

Still connected, Everett lightly shoved me backwards to the living room. After bumping into a table, prone on the couch, he burrowed under my sweatshirt to hover and press his lips along a route that went up to my chest. I was about to pull off my clothes, the excitement softened by a feeling of relaxation, what with no housekeepers or woodland creatures to interrupt us.

But then Everett pulled himself from me, peeled off his own clothes down to his underwear and socks, and to my surprise and disappointment, began digging into his duffel bag.

"Where are we...?"

"Sleeping? Right there." He nodded toward me and the couch, then extracted some other clothes from his bag.

"Oh."

"We could get a hotel room, but I doubt they offer credit to minors."

"Right."

"Are you disappointed?"

"No, I'm not. It's just…"

"What?"

"Nothing. It's fine." I patted the couch. It would do, except of course for any moment that his sister would walk out the nearby door of what I assumed was her bedroom.

Seeing my glance, he added, "It's cool. She zones out with music and headphones before falling asleep. I used to sneak up on her at home all the time."

For what, I wondered.

"It folds out," Everett explained, nodding again toward the couch.

"Oh," I tried to relax, but sitting in the home of someone I had yet to meet, whom I assumed knew of our imminent intimacy, left me confused. Almost everything I did with Everett left me confused, at first.

While Everett was in the bathroom, I tried to ignore the slightly erotic sound of him pissing, and set my eyes on the largest of the French painting posters. In it, mustached men in top hats and women in long skirts inhabited the rainy city along a wide cobblestone street where a horse-drawn carriage seemed to have just casually passed. What struck me was that there was nothing exactly in the center except the open street and a narrow building angled to fit a V-shaped intersection. It all appeared so calm, yet I sensed some kind of underlying tension, the bustle of an ordinary day hiding under the umbrellas of the painting's inhabitants.

I felt Everett's arms wrapping around me from behind. He said softly into my ear, "Kai boat."

"What?"

"Gustave Caillebotte. French Impressionist; actually, sort of a Realist. Big benefactor for Monet and some other impoverished painters."

"Your sister likes French art."

"She spent a year abroad before dropping out of college altogether. Came back with lots of trendy clothes, tubes full of posters, and a fetus."

"What?"

"The parents were scandalized, of course. They didn't want a bastard frog ruining her chances of a real marriage, and she didn't want the little tadpole either."

"I don't really think I need to–"

"Abortion, *le scandale de la famille*," he hissed with a bad accent. "She'd already refused a debutante ball, and the hairy hands of local boys who probably wanted to inherit Forrestville's wealth more than her hand in marriage. Ever since then, she's been the bad kid, leaving me plenty of room to misbehave."

"Dude, I don't think this is any of my–"

"Oh, don't worry. She'll tell her own version of it all before breakfast. Just pretend it's new gossip."

"Okay."

"We should go," he said.

"Go where?"

Everett sort of rolled his eyes. "Acquisition? Mary-joo-wanna?"

"I thought your sister was gonna–"

"She left the address. It'll be cool."

I wasn't so sure.

Having changed into different clothes, a hooded sweatshirt, jeans and boots that disguised any trace of the dashing appearance he'd previously maintained, he appeared to be any average young man, not the shivering horny wood elf or prep school suck-up I'd come to know in those few days. I wasn't aware of any dress code for making drug deals.

Why couldn't we just stay in, knowing his sister wouldn't be back for hours? What was he trying to prove?

"Am I okay?" I asked, barely masking my confusion.

"You're perfect." He approached me, offered a light kiss. "Shall we?"

The apartment of the mysterious pot dealer was on a small cramped side street in Lawrenceville, the working-class section on the north side of town. Row houses were stacked along a steep hill like playing cards. For some reason he didn't explain, Everett suggested I park the Plymouth down the street, and not in the empty driveway of the building which he'd pointed out as our destination.

"Just stay cool," Everett said.

"I am," I said. I wasn't.

"He'll probably offer to smoke some after we buy. It's kind of a fake social courtesy."

"Is it?" I snapped, silently vowing to refuse any offers before driving again.

"Testy." He left the car, closing the door quietly. I followed as he climbed up the porch stairs and knocked on the door. We heard the new Cheap Trick album playing inside. Everett knocked again... and again.

The inside door opened. Behind the screen door, a very tall man eyed us, wearing a T-shirt and denim vest, and what could only be described as a Yosemite Sam mustache. He could not have more fittingly played the role of the prison-worn drug dealer.

"And you are?"

"Holly's brother? Everett? She called earlier?"

Yosemite Sam hollered inside, "Holly's brother?"

Someone inside shouted consent. Without turning back to look at us, he opened the door.

The small front room was oddly empty. In what had apparently been a dining room converted into a living room, two rumpled sofas were arranged at angles, with a large circular coffee table in the middle. Various mismatched chairs were lined up along the other wall like some hastily furnished frat house.

In one of the cushier of chairs, a young woman with long hair sat, intently weaving some kind of macramé plant holder. She gave us both a glance, but didn't greet us.

Rising from the opposite sofa, a young man greeted us. With his conservative haircut, an Izod shirt, tan pants and loafers, he appeared to have just arrived from a Young Republicans meeting. Everett's change of clothes had been unnecessary.

He shook hands, and half-attempted some sort of soul hand slap with Everett. "Holly's little brother, huh?"

"Yessir."

"Where's she?"

"Oh, she had to work late."

"And this is?" Mr. Young Republican appraised me with a suspicious glance.

"Reid. He's cool."

Momentarily surprised that Everett hadn't invented a fake name for me, I waved and stood still, worried that I might fumble the pseudo-ethnic handshake.

"So, what can I do ya for?"

"Um, Holly said, a half ounce?"

"What kind?"

"Oh."

In another room, a phone rang.

"Hold on. Have a seat."

We sat close together on the other sofa. Young left the room.

For the first time, I saw Everett become uneasy. He leaned toward me, quietly singing the lyrics of the song blasting through the stereo as a sort of instruction. "Surrender, surrender, but don't give yourself away, ay."

Macramé girl smiled at us, but said nothing.

The Young Republican (I never heard his name) returned, pulled a drawer from under the coffee table and casually tossed out four medium-sized bags stuffed with pot. "We got ... some shitty local, Mexican Gold, Mexican Red, and Hawaiian. That stuff has the biggest kick."

"Oh. Same price?"

"No."

Some financial discussion ensued. I remained calm, outwardly, and by that I mean I was stock-still.

Negotiations settled, and the Gold was chosen. Everett handed over some cash. Mr. Young withdrew a large cluster of pot and placed it in a smaller plastic bag, then measured its weight on a tiny scale and handed it over. Just as Everett pocketed it, a series of loud knocks rattled the front door.

Yosemite Sam jumped to action, stomping toward the door. At the same moment, Mr. Young abruptly reached into the drawer and withdrew a large black pistol.

I visibly tensed. Everett clutched my knee, his white knuckles betraying his otherwise outward calm. Macramé girl sighed, annoyed, and retreated into a back room.

"Easy," Young soothed, hovering his palm over the gun.

Whoever Yosemite Sam met at the door was in an audibly argumentative mood.

Mommy's all right, Daddy's all right. They just seem a little weird...

"How old are you boys?"

"Nineteen," Everett blurted unconvincingly.

"How about," Young glared toward the increasingly loud discussion out front, "you boys go out the back door."

"Now?" Everett asked.

"Now. Slowly. Where are you parked?"

"Across the street," I said.

Everett glared at me.

"Go out through the yard. There's a fence with a door. Walk around the block and, well, good night."

We did, passing macramé girl in the kitchen, who was inspecting a jar of pickles.

Once in the dark back yard, our pace quickened. After closing the rusty back fence door, we ran down an alley, momentarily confused.

"Shit!" Everett hissed.

"This way."

"Wait! Just wait."

Everett checked his pockets, more concerned about the whereabouts of his purchase.

"What are you–"

"I might have to ditch it."

"We are not going back in there."

"I know. I just–"

"Come on."

"Where?"

"To the car. We are done." I jangled the car keys as a taunt.

Surprised, then near chuckling, Everett held his hands up in surrender. "Okay."

He followed as I instinctively figured out our passage from the back alley, past garbage cans, around the block. Cautiously, back onto the street, I peered nervously around the corner and saw my mother's car.

The argument on the porch continued. I remained resolute in our escape. Everett followed as we crossed the street, slowing our pace until we reached the car.

Yosemite Sam's glance past his irate customers led the attention of the two other men, one of them the loud one, to us.

"Start the car," Everett muttered.

"Is that them?" One of the men jumped from the porch steps in a bound. I scrambled to unlock my door, got in, started the car, then leaned over and pulled the other door lock up.

Everett darted inside as my limited parallel un-parking skills were further hampered by a skinny angry man who thought we were someone else. He pounded the hood. On the porch, the other man and Yosemite Sam began a sort of shoving match.

A soft metal crunch assured me that backing up any more would be prevented by the car I'd just hit. Suddenly searing with adrenaline, I abruptly veered the car out into the street, as the confused hoodlum gave the car another fist pound.

Several blocks and two run stoplights later, I glared at the rear-view mirror, then to Everett. Despite the temperature outside, his face was coated in a sheen of sweat.

"You happy?" I snapped.

"What! I didn't know—"

"You wanted an adventure. You got it."

"Just … It wasn't our fault."

"Fault? I'm not talking about fault. You—"

"I just wanted to—"

"Show off?"

"Well—"

"Just shut up."

He did, surprisingly, for a few blocks, before muttering, "I'm sorry."

I silently shrugged off his apology and kept driving.

"I gotta check the fender," I said, to break the tension.

"Let's just get back to Holly's first."

"Fine."

"…which is the other way."

Having approached a wide and empty intersection, I screeched to a halt, pulled a U-turn, spinning on a patch of ice, and raced the car in the other direction.

Everett whistled. "Well, fuck me, Starsky."

"I will."

Gripping the steering wheel, I held onto my anger for a few more blocks, finally slowing the car down to a reasonable pace.

"What?" I snapped.

Everett had been staring at me, but all along with an amused grin.

"'I will!'" he repeated, imitating my growled anger. And then he laughed, and eventually, so did I.

"After we get stoned."

"And have pizza?" Everett begged in a childlike tone.

"And have pizza."

More silence followed, until Everett began singing, softly at first, "Mommy's all right, Daddy's alright, they just seem a little weird ..."

Chapter 8

Fortunately, Holly had arrived home soon after we'd returned. Instead of feeling relaxed while alone with Everett, I felt edgy and frustrated, despite his flirty small talk and attempts to calm me.

We'd changed into more comfortable sweatpants, and for myself a T-shirt and Everett a rather cute thermal undershirt. He'd warned me that Holly's apartment could be a bit drafty. We'd waited for her arrival before stuffing the small bong with the frighteningly acquired pot. I didn't want to meet her while high, and Everett understood.

Holly turned out to be as wild, gregarious and self-aware as her younger brother, and as beautiful. Her long brown hair kept her tugging it back behind her ears. We had ordered a pizza from a flyer attached to the fridge by a magnet, which pleased her as she dug in while Everett told of our minor misadventure.

"Oh. My. God. I have to call Barry." She abruptly left for the kitchen, where it seemed the only phone was. So that was the name of Mr. Young Republican.

Promising to "clear things up," she assured us that no tattooed felons would come banging on her door, and that the gun was her dealer's way of showing off. The distant one-sided conversation in the kitchen made me wonder how much of that laughter was at our expense.

An old black-and-white Cary Grant movie set in some small town played on the television. Most of the pizza had been consumed, and Everett and I sat on the couch, which would soon be our bed. I felt a bit awkward, and the pot gave me that dizzying tingle I'd recalled from the few times I'd smoked any.

As Everett once again leaned in for a little pizza-flavored smooch, I felt a sudden rumbling in my lower intestines, and headed abruptly for the bathroom.

As I ran sink water to disguise what I knew would be a rather noisy release, I flushed the toilet, then waited for a second round. Dutifully washing my hands, and my face, then impulsively slurping down some tap water, I was dismayed to see how red my eyes had become. I looked in the cabinet for eye drops, found some, and dabbed a few drops while staring at the ceiling.

"You okay?" Everett asked as I returned to the sofa.

"Yep. Just a little peristalsis."

Holly had returned, seated on the nearby chair. "A what?"

"Sounds like a drag name," Everett joked. "Paris Talsis." The two of them burst into laughter, until I got the joke and forced a grin.

"Oh," Holly pointed at the television, having abandoned that bit of humor. "Randolph, Randolph..."

"Scott," Everett finished.

"They were lovers, you know."

I looked at the TV. "Who, that woman?" The actress was the subject of a brief argument between Cary Grant and the other man, handsome, but in a different way, rugged. They both wore tuxedos and were trying to simultaneously dance with the wide-eyed blonde.

"No, him and Cary Grant."

"No."

"Yes," Everett corrected me.

"See? You're not the first," Holly nodded toward us. I was stunned. While she obviously knew what was up between us, it seemed so casual.

Everett chuckled, spinning off a completely unrelated reminiscence between him and his sister. While I was familiar with the known behavioral changes that took place under the influence of pot, Holly and Everett's talk raced like the chatter of chipmunks, almost a secret lingo full of inside jokes.

My own buzz left me in silence while gazing at the TV screen. I longed for another scene between these two handsome actors, to see some indication of the rumors Holly and Everett had mentioned, but there were none.

After a brief moment between the leads and two parental character actors, the blonde rode off in a convertible with Cary Grant, unsure of her fate. The movie wrapped up abruptly with a traditional script-fonted *The End*.

"What about you, Reid?"

Holly had been talking to me.

"Sorry. What?"

"College plans?"

"Oh."

Everett had also turned his attention to me, only slightly distracted by a commercial. "I have to send out some applications. I might have a scholarship at Temple University."

"In...?"

"Well, my major'll probably be Geography, but I want to focus on the environment. I was thinking about Forestry at Penn State, but Philadelphia seems more interesting than State College."

"That's a bit unusual, to go to a city to study trees," Everett said. He was honestly perplexed or being sarcastic. I couldn't tell.

"Well," Holly joked. "You've already studied the forests, or one, at least."

"Bad joke, Sis." Everett grinned nevertheless.

Holly said, "You could go to Carnegie Mellon. We could be neighbors."

"They don't have the degree I want," I said, adding, "Besides, my parents can't afford that."

"Sorry." Holly gulped her soda. "So, your mom's car's okay?" Holly asked.

"Yeah, it's just a little dent," I said. "I'll make up some story; tell him I was teaching Everett how to drive."

"What?" Everett shot back. "I know how to drive."

"I thought you said you didn't have your license," I said, confused.

"Oh, that." He offered a sheepish grin. "It's nothing."

"You didn't tell him yet?" Holly eyed her brother.

Everett glared back at her, then rolled his eyes. "Actually, I did have my license, but I ... Okay, I stole my mom's car. Once."

"The Mercedes," Holly added.

"My bad boy phase." He shrugged as if it were nothing. "I was acting out after the divorce. Mom thought it would teach me a lesson to have my license taken away. It was ... stupid."

"Oh," I said. At least that small lie was finally explained.

"Anyway," Holly said, "I just want you to know you're safe here. It's cool. I love my little bro, despite his sometimes delinquent behavior, and you're his friend, and that's that."

"Thanks," I nodded, choking back a burst of emotion. Everett leaned close, gave my shoulder a few rubs.

"Just don't give him your car keys," she joked. Everett replied by tossing a crumpled paper napkin at her.

"Well, then," Holly stood, "I will retire to my room, sketch some more ridiculous costumes and dream of young love."

Before closing her bedroom door, her head popped out, "But keep it down, horn dogs."

We were alone again, somewhat.

"You want some more of anything?" Everett gestured toward the pizza and the bong.

"No, thanks."

"Okay, let's..." He made a gesture towards the table. I got up, grabbed the pizza box and cups, and took them into the kitchen as Everett pulled the table out from the sofa.

As I washed a few cups and a knife, tossed the paper napkins in the garbage, basically busying myself as Everett adjusted the sofa bed, I tried to prepare myself for what would or should happen next. Would we dance slowly like two tuxedoed gentlemen, then fall into each other's arms again? What happened after the fade to black? Our previous couplings had been so abrupt. This night should mean something more, but so far the whole trip had seemed like just a fumbled jaunt.

But when I returned to the living room, Everett had shifted things to a romantic mood. The room was darkened to only the flickering light of two candles, the TV turned off in exchange for a softly-playing James Taylor album on the stereo. The couch had become a rumpled bed. He tossed pillows onto it.

"Come 'ere."

I approached him, ready, I hoped.

In our socked feet, he led me in a swaying slow dance until the tents in our sweatpants bumped together too often to ignore. He then simply sat with me on the sofa and slid under the covers, smiling, anticipating, and I joined him.

While the room's heater kept the slight draft from the large windows at bay, the high ceilings of the living room left me feeling exposed. I tried to ignore Holly's proximity behind her bedroom door, tried to remember that this was our third time. A charm?

I let Everett lead me, and he knew that he should. We hugged and kissed, caressed faces and chests, pulling shirts up, sweatpants down, pushing our skin close together under the blankets and a sheet that kept getting caught under our feet.

His mouth trailed over my chest, down toward the fuzzy parts around my erection, his lips enveloping it slowly, before moving downward to my thighs. My hands awkwardly grasped at any bump and crevasse of his smaller body and its little muscled curves, awaiting a turn to reciprocate what he did to me.

"Your legs are so long," he whispered as he caressed my thigh. "Like a giraffe."

"Uh, thanks?"

"I feel like Curious George climbing all over you."

He was a bit simian, I noticed as I once again felt the tufts of dark hair between his legs, and the beginnings of a fuzzy trail from his belly to his groin. My leaner and longer body surrounded him, my tapered fingers caressing the ridges of muscle at his waist.

"Wait," he whispered as he untangled his sweatpants, pulled them off, then leaned over the sofa bed to forage in his duffel bag for a small tube. I heard a squishy sound. Everett bashfully smirked as he seemed to wipe his butt. He leaned over again, and in the shaft of a streetlight, combined with the candle glow, his buttocks rose, and I understood what we were about to do.

Placing a small towel underneath himself, Everett lay on his belly, turned back to grasp my cock, then aimed it toward himself. After tugging the covers over our bodies, I positioned myself closer.

"Just lay on top, first," he whispered.

"I never…"

"I know. You'll figure it out."

But first, I did what I wanted. The pot had settled, no longer inducing the antsy itch. I felt free to indulge, to caress his back, to hold the mounds of flesh and toy with the dark wisps of hair between them. My fingers, sticky from the lubricant, burrowed lightly. Everett raised his hips in response. "Come on, Starsky. You promised."

I pressed myself atop him, concentrated kisses on the few slight freckles along his shoulders, the nape of his neck, his ear, the side of his face as he turned, opening his mouth for a sideways kiss that became a shared soft humming between us as I slowly began to grind my hips above his.

Nudge by nudge, I dabbed, then poked, then retreated, then slid in, then out, overwhelmed with the sensation of his muscles clamping around me, then releasing, relenting as I slid further inside him. I found myself needing to think not of him, looking up at those reserved French people in the poster on the wall above us. Thrusting with too much intensity, realizing I finally had some power over him, I tried to hold off, wanting it to last, to grab some kind of memory before it all dissolved.

The album had finished before I did. The slight squeaking sound of the sofa bed amid the silence made me starkly aware of what we were doing. Abruptly, Everett shoved himself out from under me, rolled over, repositioned his legs, wrapping them around my hips, guiding me back inside him.

The covers had slid off us, but being exposed made it more intense. The shock of looking eye to eye, of kissing him, arching my back up to clearly see his face under tousled hair, and his own strokes to himself, assured me. Now, remember this, burn this into your racing heart, ignore all else but his almost proud smile and his panting breath.

With a gasp, he unleashed on himself. I followed inside of him, and the wet puddles glued us together as I collapsed atop him.

His fingers grazed my back as I panted, then soon calmed. He eased me off his chest, slipped the towel from under himself, wiped some of the sweat and sperm from our skin, and repositioned us into a more comfortable sideways hug. We tugged our disheveled sweatpants back on, but remained shirtless. Under the tugged-back blankets, our mutual body heat sufficed.

His face adjacent to my own, he whispered, not exactly into my ear, but actually at my forehead, "I told you we'd be great."

"Are you always right?"

"I'm right for you."

"But when will we see each other again? I mean, what, Tuesday's school. We'll be totally separated."

"*Pro tempore.*"

"What?"

"'For the time being.' Shhh." His fingers touched my lips, then slid from my face, past my sternum, settling at my waist after a playful cupping at my groin. "Time means nothing."

I didn't believe him, but didn't argue.

Our romantic post-coital bliss was interrupted by an unpleasant odor.

"Sorry," Everett pulled the blankets off himself, fanning them as he left for the bathroom. "Tried to get by with a silent but deadly." He winced, then let rip a comical toot before padding off to the bathroom. I almost thought I heard his sister giggling from inside her room.

After some sounds in the bathroom that he managed to disguise with the running faucet –great minds think alike– he returned, momentarily bashful. I wanted to say how something so clearly human endeared him to me even more, but I guessed it would hardly be romantic to compliment his farting.

We tried to sleep, but our hands continued more aimless grazing.

"That day ... in the forest?"

"Mmm," I mumbled.

"... was like I conjured you."

"Hmm?"

"I wasn't just doing that to do it. I was hoping for someone as daring, as crazy as me. And there you were."

While I considered our meeting a mere accident of good timing, I couldn't disagree. I remembered a feeling of urgency, unlike so many times before in more reasonable seasons, since my outdoor pleasures had become almost routine. I'd never thought some other boy would consider the option, the location, as perfect. It had been purely solitary, a gesture in defiance of the thought of a potential companion.

That happy accident had led to all this. But the line of our proximity, between the field and the forest, would in a matter of days stretch further than he or I would be able to bear for long.

Chapter 9

Despite the quiet joy of being so close to him in the bed, Everett's tousling shifts and our mutual body heat had kept me half-awake for most of the night. By morning, in my drowsy state, I tried to keep still after repositioning myself alongside him, an arm slung over his side. I wanted to cherish this quiet time of our bodies touching.

But soon he rolled over, and after a bit of affectionate nuzzling he led me to the bathroom for a shared shower that led to some playful soaping and, surprisingly, Everett's almost reverent gesture of toweling me dry.

Our preparations for breakfast roused a rumpled bathrobe-wrapped Holly, who jokingly slumped into a kitchen chair like a disgruntled diner patron.

"How are my two love birds?" she said, perking up after a few sips of coffee. Everett had learned a few tips from his family housekeeper, and presented each of us with plates of scrambled eggs and buttered toast.

Holly's conversation, more of a monologue, as Everett had predicted, revolved around her version of her year spent living in Paris. We listened attentively, and at one point, Everett casually placed his hand over my own.

"You really should go sometime," she suggested.

"Oh, I could never–"

"Yes, you could," Everett said. "We could go this summer."

"Actually, I might have plans."

"Which are?" Holly sipped her coffee.

"If I get accepted at Temple, I might get a summer job at Allegheny State Park, and that's good for advanced credit."

"Keeping grizzly bears from eating the tourists?" Everett joked.

"There aren't any," I half-scowled. "Just black bears."

"I know," Everett patted my shoulder. "Really, though, what would you do?"

"Give tours, probably; lead hikes for summer school, keep the tourists from getting lost."

"Ranger Reid! Those brown uniforms are hot."

"Sounds nice," Holly said, glaring at Everett for demeaning my budding career move. "Is that your passion?" Holly asked.

I told them of my shared hobby of gardening with my mother, something I'd enjoyed even as a child. Around the time she started working, as her interest waned, mine had continued beyond our yard.

Perhaps the actual passion had been planted on a summer weekend my parents and I spent at Twin Lakes Park. Although tiny by comparison to my possible summer job, while only a few miles northwest of Greensburg, Twin Lakes was magical to my boyhood eyes.

Then ten years old, I'd become lost on some little adventure, and met a tall handsome park ranger. After calming me down by pointing out various wildflowers, he playfully scooped me up in his arms and carried me back to my parents, who hadn't even noticed my absence. They never understood why I begged them to return.

As I decided to withhold that story, I glanced at Everett. "It's funny, I think I started becoming fascinated by nature when I heard, you know, elsewhere, not from my parents, that homosexuality is unnatural. I remember asking my dad how something that existed on earth could be unnatural, when if it was a life form, didn't that make it natural? I mean, unnatural is this table talking, or a cereal bowl turning into a cat."

"Lots of animals have gay relationships," Holly said. "It's been documented."

"Exactly."

"So, you sure you can't stay over for New Year's?" Holly asked. "I've got at least three party invites. Those opera queens sure can drink!"

With the sudden rush of meeting Everett, the holiday had completely slipped my mind. For the past few years, my parents had attended an annual party given by my father's company, leaving me contentedly alone to watch other people celebrate across the world on the television until my parents arrived home, slightly buzzed and, on a few occasions, somewhat amorous.

But now, being nearly old enough to drink legally, realizing the prospect of having the house to myself that night led me to consider inviting Everett to join me.

But before I even had a chance to ask him, he said to Holly, "Mother's having her annual shindig, and I'm expected to help out."

My sudden lurch of hopeful anticipation collapsed. Everett gave me a resigned look, as if he could sense my disappointment. I said nothing.

"Well," Everett took his plate to the sink as he rose from the table, "Your other natural passion, or should I say, our flimsy ruse for this glorious visit, awaits at the museum. We should head out. I'll have to get back home before too late, help Helen prepare the whore's devores, and give my okay to what I'm sure will be another of her military-level packing efforts for school."

While I assisted in clearing the table, maintaining a casual air, I felt anxious. We had less than a day left, the last day of the year, before Everett returned to his private school an hour north, and I to my last semester of high school. The wonderful gift had arrived suddenly, a few days late for Christmas, and would be taken away as swiftly.

"Wait! Wait!" Holly called out, chasing us as we headed towards the apartment door. In her hand she held a camera.

Everett knew there would be no turning her down, and tugged me back inside. Holly commanded us to take off our coats, settle on the sofa, then instead, the chair beside the front window, "for the light," she said, pointing to a late morning sun glowing through her white window curtains.

The extent of my portrait-posing had previously been limited to holiday shots usually taken by my dad, a few team group photos and the obligatory yearbook pictures. Having Holly direct us to "act natural," as I sat crunched into the large padded chair with Everett practically in my lap, was just odd at first. Then we settled, and she took a few pictures, Everett's arm around me. At one point, I felt a light touch of moisture at my temple, and realized that Holly had caught Everett kissing me.

"Okay, that's enough," I shrugged my way up, embarrassed but quietly pleased.

Holly walked us downstairs, hugging us farewell before we left. On the porch, she still in her bathrobe, our breaths fogged in the chill as she shivered.

"Be good," she called out as we trundled down the porch stairs. "And if you can't be good..."

"Be perfectly wicked!" Everett shouted back with a farewell air-kiss.

"It's an old joke," he confided as we settled into my mom's Plymouth. Although already slightly beat up, it usually started in even the coldest of winter days.

"Your sister's great," I said appreciatively.

"Isn't she? It's amazing my ice queen of a mother and jerk of a dad popped out such a marvel."

"Two marvels," I corrected.

Everett interrupted my attempts to start the car with a hasty peck on my cheek. "So; the muv zee vum?"

"Que?"

"Muv zee vum. You know how old museums always have V's for U's?"

"You're no end of clever."

"That's why you like me."

The giant Allosaurus greeted us in the lobby with a frozen brown snarl. Herds of babbling children, mistakenly calling it a Tyrannosaurus, were led by docents, teachers and parents. They flocked around it before being shooed off to various large doorways that led to the exhibits of the Carnegie Museum. Having been taken there twice before as a youngster on two family trips, I felt a bit of that remembered childlike excitement. Being there with Everett, however, made even the giant dinosaur skeleton inconsequential.

I'd brought a small notebook and focused on a few historic floral references in the Cenozoic exhibit. The dioramas included models of various smaller creatures. The wooly mammoth skeleton that centered the exhibit interested most visitors. I focused on the obscure, how earlier variants of the angiosperms led to modern-day wildflowers, how common ferns had their own giant ancestors.

Having scanned the room and its displays while I scribbled notes, Everett returned, giving me another one of his chummy half-hugs that were proper in a public setting, but which secretly meant more.

"Giant bones all around, and you're honing in on shrubs," he chided.

"Actually, it's quite fascinating," I argued, half-seriously. "The pluvials and interpluvials, rainfall shifts, are related to glacial melt, and all those thousands and thousands of years led to what we see in any common field."

"It's hard to believe that Heidelberg Man survived while the utterly fabulous sabre-tooth tiger never made it." I forgot that Everett's private school education surpassed mine.

"We still have horses and rhinos."

"And reindeer. Come on, let's watch the kids freak out when they see Santa's sleigh-pullers as just a bunch of bones."

Sauntering in between herds of children and a few adults, the exhibits had lost some of their fascination. It was Everett's proximity, of course.

As he gazed at a diorama of a Megatherium (basically a giant sloth) and its accompanying explanatory text, I kept sneaking glances at Everett's strong profile, the pinkness of his lips when his mouth was open, a stray eyebrow hair, marveling at the memory of his face having only hours before burrowed its way between my legs. The glow of the exhibit lights reflected through the side of his dark eyes. I realized they were not at all black, but brown with slivers of green and yellow.

"What?"

"Nothing. Just admiring the miracle of evolution."

We sauntered by a doorway that was blocked off with a wall panel and a 'Temporarily Closed' sign. We'd almost passed it, when I felt Everett's hand grab my elbow.

"Come on."

I immediately knew what he was up to. I hesitated, for a moment.

Sub-Saharan murals surrounded a smaller darkened exhibit room. A few unopened crates sat next to empty plastic display shelves. Even in the dim light, the room felt somehow comforting.

Everett led me to a far corner and expectedly pulled me into a hasty embrace. Despite my initial misgivings, I dropped my notepad and returned his kiss. We shoved hands inside our clothes, not daring to unbutton anything, at first.

After a few open-mouthed sloppy kisses and some whispered gasps, I felt his hand atop my head give a gentle push.

"Here?" Another dare; if that was what it took to keep up with him, I was determined to try.

"Sure. Nobody's coming in here."

"Except you, maybe."

I knelt, fumbled for his zipper, fished out his erection and struggled to find a proper angle to take him in. He thrust toward me, his zipper scraping my cheek. I was somewhat annoyed by his forceful hand.

"Dude, you're making me pluvial," he joked.

And, in the moment between my full-mouth chuckle and his near-orgasm, the quite expected occurred.

"Is someone in here?" An elderly guard, probably used to lesser indiscretions, appeared, annoyed but not surprised. Perhaps he couldn't see clearly.

"Oh, uh, sorry," I stuttered, jumping to my feet.

Everett swiftly turned around, having flopped his coat hem over his fly before zipping up. As we rushed toward, then past, the guard, Everett blathered some insistent excuse about his friend, in spite of the room's closure, having to document the variegation of African flora for a very important thesis paper.

After a few more effusive apologies, we fast-walked ourselves back to the main lobby and outside into the bright chilly day.

Should I have scolded him, played the role of the easily shocked apprentice in comically licentious dares? Perhaps, but I didn't. We were having too much fun.

"Now, that," he declared, "was very educational. I love the Life Sciences!"

Chapter 10

"So, school."

"Yeah, school."

The spiked skyline disappeared behind us as we drove back east. Looming ahead of us, our imminent separation matched the grey skies hovering over the pine forests beside us along the highway. A real snowstorm was expected later that night, but we were driving through somewhat clear skies.

"Tell me more about Pinecrest. What's it like there?" I asked, fighting our mutual exhaustion from the two days of strange adventures, dares, a bumpy makeshift bed, and what would have been a wall of awkward silence, were it not for Everett's casual warmth. He seemed determined not to allow gloom into his life.

"It's great," he said. "I guess I can't really compare it to yours, since I never went to a public school."

He reached his hand over and rested it on my thigh. While it was not flirtatious and more of an appreciative gesture, I playfully gunned the gas pedal.

"Those legs!" Everett rubbed my thigh.

My legs are rather lanky. As a kid, I had once gone to the Carmike Cinema for a matinee of some Disney cartoons, including their version of the Ichabod Crane story. One of my childhood acquaintances, Billy Sanders, who was just part of a cluster of neighborhood kids who played together by convenient proximity, definitely lost any friend potential when after the movie he decided to nickname me Ichabod.

For years after that, I felt self-conscious about being taller than most kids my age. My ears and nose are a bit large, too. But the night before, with Everett having caressed my legs and other parts, like some kind of living statue worthy of such appreciation, I felt stronger, more self-assured.

"You're blushing."

"No, it's the heater." I reached over his arm to the dashboard, adjusted the temperature.

"So, Daddy Long-Legs, is that why you do cross country?"

"I guess. I tried basketball, some other sports in grade school. I just couldn't care, you know? Where the ball goes, who wins. It really clears my mind, the repetition, the feeling of just running. Ever since I was little, I was already running around in the woods anyway."

"Thank you for that!" Everett offered a hokey blessing to some god that resided above and beyond the car roof.

What would have happened if I had grown up with Everett? I would probably have known of him, but only seen him from a distance. The various cliques and social substrata of our school would have kept us separated anyway. He might have been just another more popular cute guy I knew more about than I should have. Gossip and stories about the smallest of events spread through my school like bee swarms.

"Are they strict?"

"No, it's really the opposite," Everett said. "I think, well, most of my schoolmates, the boarders, have to grow up faster. The day kids, they live nearby and sometimes come and go, and pay less tuition. Of course my parents..."

I understood. Money was not a problem.

"Dad went there, and I tested smart since, I dunno, kindergarten." He told of a day, not in his memory, but bragged about often by his mother, when a teacher made some request of a five-year-old Everett, who replied at length in French. He denied any sense of talent, claiming to have probably been mimicking his sister's taped lessons, which had fascinated him.

"She's really the best. But I don't–" he halted. "The way you're so relaxed with your parents; I never had that. There's a distance, and I just feel more comfortable at school. It's not like the uniforms and ties make us little zombies. There's only about a hundred-fifty guys. Everybody knows each other. We get along, but, you know, there's a kind of hierarchy; the jocks, the science brains, the equestrian boys. We call them the cowboys, even though they ride English."

"How is that different?"

He explained the more austere style in comical terms with a British accent and gestures.

"Anyway, from what I can get, the teaching is different, more close. We're asked to understand, not just memorize. Being smart is considered cool, and actually competitive, and it makes me want to study. It's good."

"You know, I don't think I ever would have met you if you'd gone to my school."

"What do you mean?" Everett asked, a bit surprised.

"It's... I'm thinking the guys you'd hang out with wouldn't be my friends."

"Well, you don't have a lacrosse team, and I can't run worth shit."

I smiled, surrendering any further explanation.

"But we did meet," he insisted.

"Collided, more like it."

"And? Aren't you happy?"

I blushed again, tried to focus on my driving despite the flood of emotion. "Yes," I muttered.

"Well, say it, my man. Say it!"

"I'm so fuckin' happy I met you!"

"Now, that's my Starsky."

I smiled, then turned back to the road ahead. "Actually, I think I'm more of a Hutch."

We drove a while, sang along to some rock songs on the radio as Everett drummed on the dashboard. I asked him if he was hungry. He suggested we just get home, warning that his mother was already 'not amused' by his little trip. "She demands her quality time, which includes giving me a nice big send-off dinner, where we actually sit down and eat together with Helen. It's kind of a tradition."

I nodded; more miles, road signs, clouds.

Asked when he might return to Greensburg, he contemplated that and what it really meant. "I don't usually come home for weekends or anything, just, you know, no car."

"Oh, right."

"What? Don't mope. Maybe you can be nice to your parents and ask to borrow this fine chariot again." He patted the dashboard, rubbing it like a pet.

"Yes, I could, although I never have for anything or anyone before you came along."

"First time's a charm."

"Or third." That time, I had to explain my meaning. "We've had sex three times."

He hadn't kept count, I thought. Perhaps this was all just a blur to him. Perhaps I was just a new wingman for his life where such adventures were normal.

"Actually, three and a half, if you count the museum," he quipped. "Anyway, we can write to each other. We can talk on the phone, whisper sweet nothings," he tickled me in the side, or tried to from outside my coat.

Would that be it? Pen pals and road trips? It was better than nothing, the space between us at least a point between one soul and another. Everett had cracked me open with those few days of joy and affection. What would I do with such feelings in his absence?

"Do you think they know?" I asked.

"Who?"

"My parents, your mom, and–"

"Well, my sister definitely knows, obviously. She's probably already dumped the sheets in a bucket of bleach. Bad joke. Anyway, probably, but they're totally in denial. But who cares? They're not gonna stop us."

"Mmm. For the time– *Pro tempore*."

"Excellent!"

We drove in silence for a while, each of us considering our future paths.

"So, I'd invite you to my house tonight, but it's really dreary; just a bunch of old Republicans getting quietly soused."

"Right."

"You have any plans?" he asked.

"Sitting at home, thinking of you."

"Oh, that's sad."

"Whatever."

"Maybe..." His face scrunched slightly, as if in a ruse of calculation.

"Yes?"

"You'll definitely be home?"

"Yeah."

"Okay. Don't hold your breath, but..."

"But what?"

"Just cross your fingers."

"Okay," I said, intrigued.

We kept the goodbyes short in his driveway, scribbled addresses and phone numbers. I didn't get out of the car, but he did lean over to offer a clumsy hug-kiss.

I watched him walk away and, as I'd hoped, or perhaps because he didn't hear me pull away, he turned, smiled and waved.

Having prepared an edited version of the odd and wonderful events from our little Pittsburgh adventure in my head on the drive home, I unfurled it for my parents without too much effusive detail. The minor fender dent was explained with relative truth, minus the motivation.

"I'm glad you had a good time," Mom said as she eyed the dormant Christmas tree. While we traditionally waited until New Year's Day to strip and remove it, she seemed eager to bid it farewell. Most of the ornaments had been put back into the boxes on the floor.

"You sure you'll be okay tonight?"

All alone, she could have added, but didn't.

"Yeah, sure," I answered. I momentarily considered asking her if Everett could stop by. But since I had no idea if he would, I felt no need to do so.

The television showed celebrations in Australia, Asia and Europe, and the crowds eagerly anticipated the countdown in Times Square. I lay on the sofa, distracted by my more abstract thoughts about the concept of time and its association with this ritual, even the concept of Gregorian calendar years based on Jesus' birthday, which, according to some, hadn't even occurred in December. I found it absurd for Jewish and Asian cultures to celebrate a day, which didn't even exist on their calendars, with fireworks and paper horns.

I hadn't noticed that the sound of one of those horns wasn't being tooted on TV, but on the other side of our porch door window. A soft tap on the glass made me turn with surprise to see him.

Everett stood under the porch light, the horn curling and uncurling from his lips, a bottle of champagne in one hand.

I stumbled off the sofa in my rush to let him in. Once again, his chilled skin met mine as I plucked the paper horn from his lips and kissed him.

"Happy New Ear," he joked.

"Oh, it's gonna be happy, alright," I said as I let him in, dragged him to my bedroom, where I peeled off his parka with a bit of the fervor from our first time together. Everett glanced around my bedroom. It was then that he remarked, "I wanna hump every surface," but then shut off the light. "I can't stay long," he said between our licks, tugs and hurried disrobing.

In my hall-lit but otherwise darkened room, we tumbled to the floor. The cheers on the television echoed distantly from the living room, and a few random hoots down the block accompanied our passion. It was as if we were rushing through a menu of positions until, my sweatpants tangled around my ankles, he abruptly parted and lifted my legs. His tongue lapped around my balls, then down to my butt. I flinched at the odd sensation of his tongue slathering around, then in me. As I relented and gasped appreciatively, I kept thinking, where did he learn this?

Approaching an all too soon overriding sensation of bliss, with just a few of his insistent tugs on my cock, he aimed his erection between my legs. But before he got more than a few insistent pokes inside me, I spurted up and onto myself. Easing my legs down, he shifted again to straddle my chest while frantically stroking himself, and aimed for my open mouth, nearly succeeding.

Stunned by the abruptness of our lust, we collapsed and clung together, panting, until he laughed, pointing at the floor.

"What?" I asked.

"We didn't even open the champagne bottle."

I clumsily stood, pulling up my sweatpants. "Let me get some glasses."

Shirtless, I headed toward the kitchen, where I foraged in the cupboard for a pair of what Mom called 'the fancy glasses.' I heard Everett running water in the bathroom.

Half-dressed as well, he approached with the bottle in one hand.

"Dude, you're all pluvial!"

"What?"

He pointed to me, grabbed a paper towel, but before wiping, delicately licked my chest and stomach until his slurps led up my neck to my face and lips. We kissed in the bright kitchen light. I hoped some neighbor might see us through the window. I wanted the world to see us.

Before I could utter a word of caution, fearing yet another explosion of fluid, Everett deftly uncorked the bottle without a drop of spillage and poured champagne into the glasses. We toasted.

"To us," he said.

"To us."

After a few sips, he poured us each another glassful, then drank it down quickly, burping with a comic flair. "I really have to go."

"But my parents won't be back for another hour."

"Yeah, but I totally snuck out and I'm already in trouble, no doubt."

"I'm sorry."

"Don't be. It was worth it."

Silently watching as he dressed, I escorted him to the porch door. To remove the evidence of our little private party, he took the bottle.

We stood at either side of the open doorway, the winter breeze blasting into the room. With a final appreciative look, he mused, "My big studly giraffe."

"My little horny monkey."

"I'll miss you."

"Me, too."

Trudging out across the snow-laden field, he turned back from a distance to hoist the bottle in salute.

My arms tightly crossed, I shivered, swaying from the champagne buzz, refusing to close the door until he became a mere speck on the white plain.

Something about New Year's Day seemed to leave the entire town silent, as if it were experiencing a collective hangover. I didn't mind. Inside, despite the weather, I felt as warm as summer.

Mom was up a bit later than usual, preparing a large breakfast of eggs, bacon and fried potato slices. I'd already quietly helped myself to a bowl of cereal, but looked forward to digging in for more. Off in the bathroom, I heard my father singing off-key in the shower. They had returned home about an hour after Everett's departure, giggling, slightly drunk and, from the quiet sounds I heard through the wall, in a very good mood.

"So, Everett's off to his school tomorrow?" Mom asked.

"Yep."

"You're going to miss him."

I blushed. Mothers have a way of seeing right into the very heart of their children, or at least mine did.

"Yep."

I thought I'd skirted around revealing too much, and sauntered away, until Mom said, "Next time he visits, ask him to take off his boots first."

I froze, turned around, and followed my mother's glance toward the living room carpet to see a few tracks of muddy footprints.

"Right."

For once, the weather predictors were correct. After dinner, light flakes had begun to tumble down outside, bringing a late helping of Christmas-style beauty to the night. I felt the urge to pull on my boots and go for a walk, when the phone rang.

"Reid? It's your friend."

A goodbye chat, I thought; emotions disguised for the nearby eavesdropping family members.

"Hello?"

"The field; five minutes," he said, and hung up.

His figure advanced from far off. My path due south, each step, each soft crunch of snow underfoot, brought him closer to me. His cheeks already flush from the cold, we embraced, chilled skin on skin, and shared a kiss.

"I love–"

"Shh." Another kiss.

We stood close, hugging silently, before he would kiss me again and walk away, backwards for a while, we two shivering, simply watching each other dissolve into darkness, living by the minute, by the snow flake.

Chapter 11
Winter, 1979

His first letter arrived a week later, followed a few days later by a box. In it lay a sweatshirt from his school. He knew to send a worn one, no doubt his, instead of some stiff gift shop version.

I never wore it outside of home, for so many reasons. What could I offer as an explanation? *No, I didn't go there, but the most gorgeous wonderful guy who I'm totally in love with sent it as a consolation prize.*

That first letter was simple, with remarkable penmanship, a somewhat arch description of his daily activities after returning to school.

So happy that Everett had written to me, I didn't know what do; write him back immediately? What to say?

Under what I swiftly took as an understood rule that any expression of my longing should be discreet, I decided to do it in rhyme.

Once did a lumberjack love a pine straighter
Than poking' for fun in the night.
But he found a young poker
Who, nights, was a stroker
And yanked a few logs for the light.

His next letter was entirely in French. I decided to check out a French 101 textbook from the school library to try to figure it out.

I want to lick ... root of desire ... nights spending ... for times of many ... river of cream ... sent to you ... dream of me ... my ass ... grabbing your ...

Basically, it was obscene. I was relieved that I'd followed my instinct not to ask my Biology lab partner, Brenda Marsh, to translate it.

Brenda was the only fellow student who had noticed my change in behavior. The previous semester, before I'd collided with Everett, I'd been pretty much the same quiet studious kid, the sandy-haired guy you sort of know in class who rarely speaks up, never stands out, who is easily ignored, but whose private world would astound.

Brenda and I had been friends since grade school. Her long strands of blond hair usually covered most of her face, except in Biology, where she tied it back while poring over a microscope or when we dissected frogs. We had spent the first part of senior year sharing conspiratorial gossip about our classmates and teachers. Apparently her French teacher Madame Pinchon had begun to have a little bladder problem, and more often left her students to chat in small circles, babbling away in French conversation.

"So, got a girlfriend?" she asked bluntly on a Tuesday after another of Everett's letters had arrived. That one had been a series of scrawled cartoons done in a few colored markers. In it, he'd been taken hostage in a sub-basement of his school, only to be saved by ReidMan, a cartoon version of me. Everett had captured my dorky look a bit too clearly; my glasses, my jug ears and my shaggy hair. In the last panel, we were making out mid-air, with my magic cape fluttering just enough to keep the drawing from being too graphic.

"Huh?" I gave Brenda a falsely quizzical return glance.

"You're like, I dunno, brighter."

"Was I dark before?"

"No, but it's like you were just filling time. Now you're diving into class. You've been raising your hand a lot, answering questions. You never used to do that."

"Well, I got a few nice surprises over the holidays," I replied, offering a hint, but no more.

"So, you did get some action."

"Is it that obvious?"

"Your skin's cleared up, for one thing."

Inspired by Brenda's having intuited my post-virginal glow, I struggled to share even a coded explanation of my affection for Everett. Words couldn't match the quiet pride I felt from knowing that he thought of me.

Our distance fed my longing. I didn't want to settle for the innuendo in our obscured lustful scribblings. Everett had hinted in a previous letter about a need for caution, that his roommate, whom he'd mentioned a few times as being nosy, might "accidentally" read his letters.

Instead of writing again, I trekked into the woods, searched out that sacrosanct area under the evergreens, yanked up a few small tufts of still green grass, scooped up some tiny pine cones, and put them in my coat pocket. Once home, I nestled the wintry souvenirs in with one of my worn T-shirts and placed it in a box. I waited for a Saturday when my mom needed a few errands done, then, in between, stopped off at the post office and sent it to him.

About a week later, a small box arrived in return. Fortunately, my parents respected my privacy and hadn't opened it. Inside a large plastic bag was one of his jock straps.

Unable to top his gift, at least in its intimate audacity, I sent him a note with a newspaper clipping, an announcement of an open half-marathon that our school would be hosting in mid-May. Lots of people competed, some for fun, but I knew many of my cross country opponents from others schools, plus my own teammates, would think of it as a competition. I wrote, "I'm having my 18th birthday party that weekend. Hope you can be here for it."

Only a few days later, he called.

I should explain the communications barrier, the situation that led to our letters and increasingly unique packages.

Everett had told me there were no phones in the dorm rooms. A bank of old telephone booths in a main hall next to their cafeteria had been updated to a somewhat antiquated system where each student could enter his own room number and have calls charged to his bill, meaning his parents' bill.

I never got the impression that Everett wanted to hide me from his mother; quite the contrary. At some point, I realized that Everett planned to use our relationship to defy his mother, in the same way his sister had done, only without the trip to France and the subsequent aborted "tadpole."

So I was a bit surprised to be awakened one Saturday morning in late February to my dad's knock on the door.

"It's your friend Everett on the phone."

Still groggy and in my usual sweatpants and T-shirt, I tried to rouse myself to absorb the pleasure of hearing his voice for the first time in weeks.

"Hello?"

"Happy birthday to you," he sang, continuing in a way that made each note sound risqué. Then, "Reid, my man, you're becoming ..."

"... a man?"

"Legal for several illicit activities. We'll both be eighteen."

"What? When is yours?"

"Oh, last week."

"Why didn't you tell me?" I wanted to share so much; that I'd visited our little meeting place in the woods at least twice a week, that I was growing out my sideburns as he'd suggested, and yet he hadn't even bothered to tell me about his birthday.

"It was no big deal. Some of the guys threw me a little party. My mom sent me some clothes. Dad just sent money and a tie."

I felt stung, left out.

"I'm gonna try my best to get down there for your big day. There's no bus, so I might hitch a ride with one of the other guys who live nearby. But I am not whining back home for any kind of limo service, so sorry if I'm late but–"

"Dude, dude, dude; I'll pick you up wherever. Yes, that'd be great. I wanna ..."

"What?"

"I wanna see you soon, you know?"

"I don't know when, but yes, we will," Everett said. "Hey, before that; what are you doing ... wait, March twenty-something, third Saturday, I think?"

"I have no idea."

"My mom's head of the committee for the country club's annual shindig."

"Shindig?"

The Forrestville Country Club was an exclusive yet small estate set just across the county road from the wealthy neighborhood. Behind it, the sprawling expanse of the private golf course was opened to non-members for winter sledding.

"Yeah, the Spring Fling," Everett continued. "It's this corny benefit they throw every year, sort of a parent-kid party, like *American Bandstand* meets *The Lawrence Welk Show*. The old folks party with the kids. Mom turned it into this fancy fundraiser kid's charity, like, before I was born. You don't have to bring a date, like a girl, or anything."

"I would hope you'd be my date."

"That's the plan. You can help me celebrate my eighteenth, a little late."

"Okay. But, wait; do my parents get invited?"

"Uh, they don't have to. Do you want them there?"

"I guess, unless this really is a date?"

"Yeah. We can duck my parents after dinner. Besides, kids get in free, even though we're not officially kids anymore. The tickets are two hundred bucks."

"Oh. Then, no to the parents."

"Okay. I'm guessing you don't have a tux."

"No. I have a suit."

I'd rarely worn it; most recently at a funeral for a distant aunt I'd only met a few times. I had stared at it in the car on the drive to my uncle and aunt's home as it swayed on a little hook over a side window. Like most teenagers, I was uncomfortable with the mere idea of a tie and suit.

An image flashed in my mind, a version of that Cary Grant and Randolph Scott movie we'd half-watched that night at Holly's. Would Everett take me in his arms, whirl me around the dance floor, defying and shocking an entire community of Forrestville's wealthy elite? Would he propose on bended knee?

None of that would happen, exactly, but we would rather clearly exhibit our affection, and with our bow ties still on.

Chapter 12

The Polaroid upset me.

He attached a note, calling it 'an early birthday present.'

In it, Everett posed, arms and little biceps flexed, the biceps I'd kissed, licked, nibbled on.

The Polaroid.

In it, Everett grinned with mischief, wearing only white undershorts.

In it, the bulge in those shorts showed a level of interest; not rigidly excited, just turgid.

It's a joke, I told myself. Someone took it and he knew I'd get off on it. I did, several times.

But that pleasure began to blend in with the mental burn from an unanswered question. If Everett was running around with a chubby getting his picture taken, then who took the picture?

Polaroids didn't have time delay settings, did they?

While I, an hour away, longed and pined for him even more as Everett sent these letters and packages, some other guy got to be with him, underwear close, boner close, shirtless little biceps-flexing close.

I sent him some generic birthday card I'd foraged from my mom's collection, but refused to mention the photo.

A few weeks passed, and I heard nothing from Everett.

School became actually more relaxed, despite the rumbling internal engine of wondering what he was doing, how often he thought of me, and when I would see him next. I let it settle into a sort of comfort. Adored by him, I would be again, I hoped. Perhaps having no prior romantic experience was my saving grace. Perhaps I was just a fool.

Seeing couples holding hands in the school hallways, all opposite-sex pairs, of course, no longer annoyed me. I have that, too, I told myself. But it's so special it can't be shared casually between geometry and gym. So what if its consummation required sometimes difficult and unusual locales?

Then, postcards began to arrive almost daily, each with one word.

SEVENTEEN
YOU
GOING
ARE
ON

The images weren't unusual; pastoral Pennsylvania, Amish farmlands, a few depicting his school. They weren't the point. It wasn't until most of them arrived that I figured out, of course, that they had an order. Everett was cleverly doling out our cryptic secrets, displaying them for the world, or at least the postman. My mother, who had politely left them on my bedroom desk, barely withheld her own curiosity.

One of the postcards arrived on a Saturday.

"Why is there only one word on this?" Dad said that day as he handed it to me while sorting bills.

"It's kind of a running joke I have with Everett," I said as I glanced at another corny autumnal image, and written on the other side, BABY.

I'd pieced together that Everett had written the first lyrics from the song in *The Sound of Music* where the cute Nazi bike messenger and the older daughter get to sing and dance and make out in a gazebo on a rainy night.

I knew with every postcard Everett imagined just such a gazebo, except we were two cute little bike messengers, without the girl, or the Nazis, or even the bike, but definitely the rain.

Outdoors in the rain; we'd have to try that some day.

Chapter 13

"Hey, Reid, ya got a minute?"

Actually, I had half an hour, since it was lunch period and I was sitting alone at a table, eating.

"Sure, Kevin. What's up?"

Kevin Muir's kiana shirt, a wide-collared profusion of lime green and hot pink swirls, clung tightly to his muscled chest. His jeans, bell-bottoms wide at the cuff, held tightly to his waist, pressing out in the expected areas.

He sat down across the table from me with his tray of food. Like me, he had cut his hair short for fall training, but it had grown out to the typical long style similar to mine. Unlike me, Kevin was popular and knew it, but he didn't lord it over anyone. One of the aforementioned cool dudes from the track team, he drove us in his van to the rock concerts (Kansas, Electric Light Orchestra, and Foreigner). A pretty amazing pole vaulter, and one of few guys at school who could get away with such daring outfits, Kevin Muir was beyond criticism.

"I was wondering if you wanna do distance for the track team again."

"Oh. I don't think so," I said.

"Well, you know, Shot's gone, so we're short a man."

'Shot' was Gary Hendershott, who had become a bit too intimate with his girlfriend, Tammy Krebs. He usually ran a good second at most distance events, did better in the two-kilometer races. He'd dropped out and gotten a GED since becoming an expectant father rushed into becoming a husband. His sudden disappearance, similar to that of a few other students each year, became the subject of a lot of gossip. The stories had left me more relieved than isolated for being the only gay guy I knew of at school, other than a few of the kids in the Drama Club.

"I dunno, Kevin. I'm kind of focusing on my SATs and college, you know? I mean, I'm training a bit for the half-marathon in May, but that's just for fun." Actually, encouraged by Everett's upcoming visit, I had been training on my own more than usual. I wanted to place well for him to witness.

What I didn't say was that while the track team's distance runners were an okay bunch, some of the others, sprinters and field guys, thought of themselves as rock stars, and acted like it.

In my sophomore year, I had joined the track team the spring after my previous meager success in the fall cross country season. I didn't consider the track antics, mostly comprised of homophobic names and swearing, to be any sort of threat, just annoying.

With the guys on cross country, there wasn't any locker room banter because we usually just went home to shower, at least at home meets. We didn't travel as a pack on school buses, just a few cars. Distance runners had nothing to prove. We were usually too exhausted to bother anyone else.

Kevin was an exception, one of the most casually popular guys I knew from the track team. His father owned the largest car dealership in the county. Muir

Autos billboards welcomed drivers to Greensburg at each of the town's major entry roads with the catchy phrase, 'Get More at Muir!'

Yet Kevin wore his elite status with a cool resolve, always greeting me in the hallways if he wasn't too distracted by his latest girlfriend. His family lived in Forrestville, just down the secluded street from Everett's family. That Everett had mentioned being his childhood friend made me see him in a new light.

"Come on, you're good," Kevin said. "Besides, you're getting a bit chunky, doncha think?"

It was an old joke, how the loosely knit clan of rangy runners would complain about gaining an ounce or two, as if we were supermodels.

"I'll have to think about it. When's training start?"

"Two weeks. But we got some indoor training goin' on at the college."

The local branch of Penn State had open days at an indoor track. The ramps and humming florescent lights annoyed me. When I had trained there as a sophomore, I toyed with lapping straight-aways with my eyes closed, just so I could pretend I was running outdoors, which was my original reason for joining cross country.

"I'll think about it."

"I'll teach ya how to pole vault," Kevin teased.

Part of our coach's spirited early training my sophomore year had involved his encouraging all new guys to try events they hadn't done before. The only requirement for attempting pole vault was putting on a smelly old scraped communal football helmet. Despite the advantage of using pole vault as a way of befriending him, I passed then as well.

"No thanks. I prefer my skull in its original shape."

I couldn't deny that watching Kevin compete in pole vault was fascinating. What beguiled me, and no doubt a few others, was the frequency of his jock strap bulge – and occasionally some of its contents– popping out of his shorts mid-leap.

Kevin talked about some other things, but those memories of him stuck. Under the table, I furtively adjusted the pronounced tightening in my pants. I wondered if he actually wanted to strike up a friendship, or if any of that was just a ruse to get me to join the track team.

I wanted to mention Everett, but knew that our little romance would at least be deduced by him, if not admitted by me. But more important, the mere mention of our connection, there in the school cafeteria, felt out of place.

Instead of parting ways, we chatted until the bell rang. As we left, Kevin added, with an oddly affectionate shoulder pat, "Think about what I said."

Up until then, I hadn't thought much about deception, or false intimacy, or any kind of second-guessing of people. But with Everett in my life, or at least in my memory and mailbox, I had begun to consider the ulterior motives of other people.

Chapter 13
Spring, 1979

You are cordially invited on behalf of:
The Forrester Family
To attend the Greensburg Annual Spring Fling!
Saturday, March 24
At the Forrestville Country Club
Formal Attire
Send RSVPs to:

A phone number and a mailing address followed. Even though Everett said I was already invited, I figured this was a formality, it being a formal event. I cautiously checked the 'Yes, I Will Attend' line and inserted the tiny reply card into its tiny envelope.

That had been a few weeks before my trip downtown to try on a rental tux. Everett had sounded a little snippy when I'd again asked if I could just wear my dark suit. "No, a white dinner jacket. You can get one at Troutman's downtown."

Fortunately, Mom agreed. She'd also eventually agreed that on the night of the benefit, she and my father would decide to have other plans.

Troutman's was out of white dinner jackets, there being a rush on them in advance of the gala. The polite saleslady on the phone suggested Lapels, "A Fine Men's Clothier," on South Pennsylvania Avenue. I'd been to the Sears down the block several years before with Mom to buy my black suit. I discovered upon trying it on that it had become clownishly short on me.

With five crisp twenties in my pocketed running pants, I donned my hooded sweatshirt and headed out to take Mom's car downtown. Her enthusiastic cheerfulness took an annoying turn.

"Are you sure you want to wear that?"

"Mom, I'm renting a tux, not interviewing for a job."

Like a lot of mid-sized Pennsylvania towns, Greensburg is nestled around a set of hills that give it a cozy feeling, while also making for frequent flooding. Several days of early spring rain had let up, but a clammy dampness clung to the wet streets.

Almost every building, from the train station Clock Tower to the rows of shops, and most of the department stores and banks, were made of red brick, with fixtures done in Romanesque or Italianate Revival style. It's actually quite pretty, like a middle-aged librarian who might still someday get a date.

My mother had been right, in a way. The stout clerk took a glance at my tracksuit, a bit too quickly greeted me inside Lapels, almost determined to shoo me away to the Sears down the road.

"May I help you?"

"Yes, I, uh, called about renting a tux; a white dinner jacket."

"And when would you need this?"

"The Saturday after next. The Spring Fling at the–"

"Oh. Oh, yes, certainly."

That changed his attitude. He must have assumed I was the indolent son of one of Forrestville's wealthy locals. I more clearly understood Everett's behavior, how he just expected things to go his way, and how they usually did.

After taking a few measurements of my arms and shoulders, he sorted through his rental tuxedos from a rack toward the rear of the shop. I tried on a few of his suggestions, not knowing what to look for.

"The cuff is still a bit short. Here," he fussed, and a third was offered.

While it looked a bit odd over my grey T-shirt, as I glanced at myself in a full-length mirror, I began to see the illusion of elegance taking place on my lean frame.

"Yeah, this is good, right?"

"Certainly." He fussed about me, brushing off my shoulders, tugging the sleeves down just so. I felt a flush of embarrassment at his touch, and made a sudden realization that there were quite possibly other gay men· in Greensburg, other people who longed for a guy with a charming smile. While certainly I had wondered, I'd never clearly realized the actual possibility.

"Will there be anything else?"

"Yes," I said with a newfound assuredness. "Some black pants, a white shirt, and a black bow tie."

My parents had made good with their 'other plans' by hightailing it to a movie. Everett had called the night before when he arrived from school, more concerned about my apparel than making plans to meet before the gala ("Sorry. Family time.") or on Sunday afterward ("Hopefully").

Finally dressed for the night, alone in the house, I felt awkward, like an albino penguin, afraid to lean back in the chair. Why was I doing this, just to please Everett? To impress his parents as he had done mine? Couldn't we just sneak off to the woods?

The doorbell rang. I nervously jumped up to open the door.

Everett looked absolutely dashing in his own white dinner jacket, perky black bow tie, and a smile that dazzled. I finally understood why girls at school became so starry-eyed over a prom date.

"Giraffe!"

"Hey, Monkey," I smiled.

"You look great!"

"Thanks. You, too."

"You ready?"

"I guess I'd better be."

"Our ride awaits."

With the introductions and handshakes made in the car, Everett and I sat in the back as Carl and Diana Forrester behaved most unlike a divorced couple, in fact downright cheerful. My 'date' and I furtively held hands in the back seat, occasionally finger-fighting like mating spiders.

Our hands abruptly parted when Mrs. Forrester turned to give me a speculative glance.

"I'm so sorry your parents weren't able to attend tonight," she said.

"Yes, um–"

"I've been planning this event for simply months, and this little detour isn't a bother, but still, if I can allow myself a moment of immodesty, it is the event of the season. Do you dance?"

"Excuse me?"

Everett rolled his eyes.

"Dancing. There are so many young ladies your age who would so appreciate it. It is the thing to do, especially since you're without ... female escorts. Have you been to the club?"

"Uh, just in the winter, Ma'am; sledding."

"Oh, yes. It's so nice that the staff shares the property on occasion." As she continued on about the event's history, she turned back to check her appearance in the passenger seat visor's drop-down mirror.

I felt a playful finger poke at my side. Everett's comically contorted face forced me to stifle a burst of laughter.

The event proved to be everything Everett described, a somewhat old-fashioned wedding reception, but without the wedding.

The white tux made my black-rimmed glasses more noticeable. Some older guest told me I looked like Buddy Holly. That probably had more to do with the movie about the singer having been released the year before. When I decided to joke, "Actually, I was going for Elvis Costello," it fell flat, and the gentleman turned away with a vague smile.

Grandfathers danced with young girls and mothers danced with their sons, but mostly the kids hung around the edges of the ballroom while their parents cautiously partnered through rumbas and waltzes. Fragrant floral displays at each table gave the room a festive air and a heady scent.

As dinner was served, the band on a small stage in the ballroom took a short break, leaving one lone pianist. He tickled out a medley of songs, the tunes of which were all familiar but unnamable to me.

"Actually, this is the fifty-third Spring Fling," Mrs. Forrester said with a hint of familial pride after we settled to our table at the center of the dining room. Two other older couples were also at the table. Everett and I were briefly introduced. I promptly forgot their names, and they politely ignored us.

A small army of waiters appeared with plates, serving our table first. My limited experience with formal dining (a cousin's wedding in Scranton and our grandparents' fiftieth wedding anniversary) told me that this meant something. The Forresters, divorce or no, still had status.

Everett's mother led our table conversation with more of a historic lecture from across a floral centerpiece which, compared to my woodland preferences, was almost psychedelic.

"Carl's great-grandfather Isaac Forrester inaugurated the gala in 1926 by celebrating the completion of the original club, a much smaller building, but set on the same property."

"Which burned to the ground in 1937," Mr. Forrester added with a sardonic grin. "Kitchen grease fire."

Mrs. Forrester shot her ex-husband a glare as Everett and I stifled laughter over our plates. She continued her lecture to the others.

Everett leaned in and muttered to me, "Start scoping out a girl to ask to dance once or twice."

I gave him a quizzical stare, then discretely glanced about the room. A few girls our age sat alertly at their parents' tables. I heard a laugh behind me, and saw one girl with braces and glasses. Yes, definitely. As I had for those few school dances, I could do this again, this little lie, the pretext of heterosexuality, with him.

"Target acquired," I nudged to Everett.

He glanced, withheld a snort, and muttered, "Ellen Hodge."

After a smattering of applause amid the light clatter of dinner plates being removed, a few people resumed a place on the dance floor.

"That's my favorite Cole Porter song," Mrs. Forrester announced. "Did you know, he fell off a horse and was paralyzed for a great part of his life."

"I did not know that," one of the other guests said.

"He wrote some of his best musicals after that. Remember when we went to see that production of *Kiss Me, Kate*?"

"I do," her ex-husband chimed in.

"And then, he didn't," Everett grumbled. He and his father shared mutual silent glares.

Fed up with the entire situation, Everett abruptly rose and announced, "Well, we'll let you all stroll down Memory Lane," then nodded for me to accompany him. "As requested, Reid and I are going to see if a few of the young ladies might like to dance."

"Oh! How nice of you," Mrs. Forrester said, in a tone that made me wonder if this family ever spoke to each other without an undercurrent of sarcasm.

The girls were surprised and giddy. Ellen kept glancing past my shoulder to see who was watching her dance with me, as if one slow dance with a boy might solve some unspoken self-esteem problems. We chatted in between my clumsy footwork. When I mentioned that I was Everett's guest, she seemed impressed, and perhaps a bit jealous that he'd chosen her friend.

After our one slow dance, Everett and I were about to thank our partners and excuse ourselves, when the bandleader stepped up to a microphone and announced a "kids only" dance. "Let's shake it up a little," he said, attempting a sort of joke.

The band's rendition of "Stayin' Alive" was an even greater joke. The girls attempted to shake their hips and get into it, but were clearly unprepared, as was I.

But then I noticed Everett's arm nearly poking me, and he turned to me with that mischievous grin, some rather suggestive hip thrusts, and a hoot of, "Get it goin', Reid!" A sort of disco dance-off ensued, the girls stepped back, and before I knew it, he and I were sort of dancing together.

That the band proceeded into "I'm Your Boogie Man" only got more kids onto the dance floor, and my duet with Everett became less obvious. I sought out Ellen and waved her back, but she smiled and held up her hands in surrender.

As the song reached its end, Everett dragged me to the girls for a thank you bow, took me by the elbow, sweat beginning to glisten on his brow, and led me toward a back exit beside the stage. On the way, he grabbed an open bottle of red wine from a serving tray.

"Where are you taking me?"

"Under the stars, for our real date."

Traipsing off into the expansive back lawn of the club's golf course, Everett stopped by a cluster of trees, gulped down some wine, and gestured for me to follow. His dares were taking on a different tactic. I wasn't sure how much a part I was playing in it all, other than as an accessory.

Huddled in our newly found hiding place, Everett handed me the bottle. I took a swig, careful not to spill any wine on my tux, but less concerned when he casually leaned against a tree trunk. His jacket wasn't a rental.

"Come 'ere, handsome."

"That was so fun, dancing with you," I said as we drew closer. We took turns kissing and finishing off the bottle before I set it on the ground.

Everett's hand dug inside my jacket. He stroked up and down my torso, then abruptly pulled my shirt up. His cold hands made contact with my stomach, my chest, inducing shivers as we kissed. It was sloppy, urgent, sweetened by the wine, interrupted by a few burps and resultant giggles.

"A lil warmer this time, huh?" Everett smiled as he reached down into my pants to grasp what had been jutting against his thigh. I returned the gesture, dug into his shorts, kissed him from his lips, chin, jaw, and down his neck to just above his bow tie, which I also kissed.

I parted my legs to keep my pants from completely falling to the moist lawn. Everett yanked my shorts down, letting my dick spring free, and was about to kneel, or crouch, probably, when we heard a voice.

"Boys?"

Everett froze, jerked his head around. I turned to see his father standing in a surprisingly casual stance.

"How about you zip up, wash your hands, and come on back inside, okay?"

"Sorry," Everett said, yanking his pants up as we both turned away.

"No, you're not. Make it snappy."

"How did you–"

"One of the kitchen guys saw you leave with a bottle; thought he ought to tell me."

"Damn," he muttered.

"Yeah. And the next time you think you're hiding out, you might not do it in white jackets in the moonlight."

Mr. Forrester turned away, preceding us back toward the club.

"Fuck!" I hissed at Everett.

"Well, not this time."

In the men's room, after making sure we were alone, Everett tried to calm me down. "It's okay. He won't–"

"Won't what? Why do you always–"

"Oh, like you didn't want to?"

"No. Yes. But it's not–" I hesitated, dizzy, realizing I was a bit drunk.

"What? Not right?" Everett snarled as he turned away to check himself in the mirror.

"Yes, it's right to do," I stammered. "It's right for us to … but it's like you wanted to get caught."

"So?"

"Dude. I'm here, too. Let me decide when I do that."

"Okay. I get it. Sorry." Everett's comic glance lightened me up enough to accept his rushed apology kiss. "But remember; you came with me, willingly."

"A few more minutes, and we would have."

He snorted a chuckle as he fixed my tie.

As we headed out, he said, "Besides, the rich girls in this crowd get parties thrown for them when they're ready to put out."

"So?"

He patted my butt. "You just helped me celebrate my coming out ball."

Chapter 15

Through the thankfully brief ride home, Mrs. Forrester, aided by a few drinks, acted more than cheerful, apparently as yet uninformed of our little escapade. Everett's father dropped me off with a curt, "Good night," while from the back seat, Everett offered nothing but a parting wink.

Back inside the house, I slumped onto the couch, my tux in slight disarray like some junior James Bond. The combination of alcohol and Everett's inspiring brash actions sparked my moment of bravery.

My father turned his attention away from a book and the softly playing Herb Alpert record as I sighed, "I'm in love."

"Are you now?"

Despite the late hour, I had his attention, and figured I might as well head off any upcoming gossip or crisis. Mr. Forrester would probably want to talk with my dad, or beat him up, or do whatever fathers do. Since my father had never been in such a situation with me, it seemed sensible to prepare him.

"You met a girl tonight?" He spoke softly. Mom was asleep in their bedroom, I guessed.

"No, Dad."

"You met a girl some other night and she was there."

"Dad. There is no girl in the equation."

"You're drunk."

"A bit, but that's beside the point."

"Okay." He turned the music down a little, looked down the hallway, as if expecting Mom to enter with perfect timing to relieve him of this sudden parental duty. A quizzical frown came over him, like when he'd sit hunched over the dining room table doing some after-work accounting while piecing together old cardboard jigsaw puzzles to break up the monotony.

He wouldn't erupt in hatred or rage. I knew that. He wasn't a religious man, or a bigoted man, but merely a calm intelligent soul who had just realized that the missing puzzle piece was right in front of him.

"Your little friend, the Forrester kid."

"Bingo." And then my eyes welled up, perhaps from the drink, with a happy sort of relief that I was sharing the knowledge of this bundled up joy.

"Huh. Well, gosh, Reid. Are you … Are you okay?"

"Yeah, Dad."

"I mean, is he … Does he know? Has he … reciprocated?"

"Oh, yeah."

"Well, you know we love you. Should I get your mother?"

"No, no. I just wan' you to know, because–"

"Well, of course I'd want to know. For a while back there, we thought you weren't even … I mean, good. He's being nice to you?"

"Oh, yeah. We definitely resifripated."

Dad withheld a chuckle. "You've been, I dunno, a little different lately, but happier. I thought he was just your friend, but I guess I wasn't even looking."

"There is this ... situation. We kinda got caught makin' out tonight, so, I just wanted to give you a heads up, in case it gets around."

"Oh. Is that going to be a problem?"

"Well, I don't think I'll be invited back to the country club any time soon."

"Darn."

"Only one person caught us."

"Oh, good."

"Everett's dad."

"Not so good."

"Yeah. So, anyway..." I stood up, swaying. He stood up to catch me. It became an awkward brief hug.

"You sure you don't want to wake your mother, talk to her?"

"No, I think she's already figured it out."

"Oh."

"Yeah. G'night Dad."

"Good night?"

I didn't remember taking off my tux and hanging it up so neatly before passing out in my bed, but I did. At least I think I did. I didn't wake up until my mother barged into my bedroom around noon.

"Telephone. Your ___friend, Everett."

She said it exactly like that, pausing where she could have said 'boy.' Dad had obviously had a follow-up conversation that morning as I slept off my hangover. I think my mother was more upset that I hadn't come out to her first.

Groggy and queasy, in a T-shirt, some sweatpants over the previous night's shorts and my itchy black socks, I followed her into the kitchen and picked up the phone.

"I'm totally grounded," Everett growled.

"Dude," I whispered, "is your dad gonna–"

"Him? No, don't worry. He's ... Don't worry about it. Dad and my mom had a big fight about something else, and I'm in trouble by extension, plus the drinking, so I can't see you today and I gotta head back to school tonight. My dad's got chauffeur duties, even though it's two hours out of his way." A bit of silence, then, "So, anyway, we had fun, yeah?"

I felt a lurch in my stomach, as if his saying 'had fun' meant there wouldn't be any more.

"Yeah. Yes, we did." And then, impulsively, I said it, attempting to sound casual. "What if I drove up to your school?"

"What?"

"Come up and visit you."

"Oh. Um..."

"Forget it. Stupid idea."

"No, no, it's ... Sure. This weekend's no good. We have a home game Saturday after next. They have guest dorms, but we'll figure something out."

I assumed he meant that we would have to concoct some clandestine scheme to make out in private, if at all. But more than that, I couldn't understand how he could be so casual, let alone not hung over. Would my visiting mean anything? Would it mean too much?

"You think your parents'll be cool with it?" Everett asked.

Recalling my drunken confessions of the previous night, I snuck a peek around the hallway toward the kitchen and living room. While Mom angrily scrubbed some surface, Dad calmly read the Sunday paper.

"Fifty-fifty chance."

"I like those odds," he said. "Gotta go. I'll call you with directions in a few days."

I didn't tell him I knew exactly where his school was –twenty-nine miles north– having looked it up on a state road map.

The next week, the Three Mile Island nuclear power plant nearly blew up on the other side of Pennsylvania. People starting talking about panicking, but nobody panicked. Gas lines got longer, then shortened. My dad held some serious discussions with some business associates most evenings about their truck drivers. The news on television and in the papers honed in on our state in a somewhat gruesome fascination with the near-disaster area that it was.

I thought about doing an extra credit paper for Biology on the potential effects of nuclear fallout on the environment, but I couldn't muster any interest. I didn't expect my level of apathy, nor did my parents.

"I would think you would care more, with your interest in nature," Mom said over a humorless dinner.

"Actually, I do. It's just, if we're going to all die of radiation, I'd like to have one more visit with my, uh, ___friend."

What I didn't expect was my mom allowing my visit, but then only a day beforehand telling me she needed her car. She seemed upset about something, that something being me.

I told her that was fine, I would simply take a bus and jog the rest of the way. They didn't know I was bluffing, that there were no buses to Saltsburg. Despite that, and in spite of my mother, Dad casually tossed me his car keys.

I'm pretty sure it was all good timing that I was leaving for a day, because for the first time in years, my parents were about to have an argument.

Chapter 16

A brick castled estate, a miniature fortress, a quaint campus, a beguiling maze of handsome young men in jackets and ties, Pinecrest Academy for Boys fulfilled most of my expectations. While the campus was a bit smaller than I'd expected, it had the look of prep authenticity.

Everett told me to just meet him on the field, but by the time I arrived, the players were already warming up. Less than fifty fans sat in the bleachers, somewhat arranged in clusters for one team or the other. Being a home game, most of those fans were Pinecrest students and a few parents.

Although I had expressed my disinterest in team sports, specifically ones which involve a ball of some kind being tossed back and forth, because it was Everett's sport, I had done a little research and checked out a book about it from the library. Discovering that its heritage stemmed from Native American history going back centuries made the game appear less odd and more of an underdog sport.

Everett raced across the field in his shorts, jersey, gloves and a helmet that resembled a motorcycle-football hybrid. His schoolmates hooted and hollered for their every goal and turnover as I sat quietly, marveling at Everett's every leap and jump. Watching any other game would have left me unfazed. But with Everett on the field, I found myself rapt by following his every move. The somewhat revealing shorts helped.

More than a few times, though, some rough hits knocked players to the ground in a surprisingly violent manner. Players were frequently fouled, and it didn't let up until the final minutes as Pinecrest trounced the opposing private school team by several points.

After his jovial backslapping herd of teammates left to change in the locker room, Everett sought me out in the stands. I stepped off the bleachers.

"Whadja think?" he said, beaming as he pulled off his helmet.

I thought not to make any overt gesture of affection, but before I knew it, his sweaty body wrapped itself around me. Returning with a congratulatory hug, his shoulder pads crunched against my chest.

"Excellent. It was really exciting."

"Coming from you, that means a lot."

A few other boys interrupted our moment together with more hugs and hoots. I pulled back, admiring it all, yet knowing I was out of their circle of athletic joy. My own experience with cross country rarely involved cheering, instead runners finding a bit of grass upon which to kneel, collapse or vomit.

"Be back in a bit," Everett tossed off as he left.

Waiting for him in the bleachers as students and families departed, I gazed out over the nearly empty field. One of the team assistants picked up various stray paper cups near the benches, along with a water cooler and a few shin guards. At one point, his arms too full of objects, he tripped on the side of a bench and fell flat on his back.

The celebratory informal pizza party was held in a game room in one of the dorm buildings. Everett's teammates made cheerful and surprisingly non-obscene jokes, some of which I didn't understand, because they were in Latin, fewer of which were explained to me.

Seated at the room's edge, I was an anomaly, a politely welcomed outsider, just "Ev's buddy." The lone guy not wearing a button-down shirt and loosened tie, I felt a bit out of place. There appeared to be a silent understanding, that the truth of our intimacy was possibly known but not mentioned by them.

For some reason, Everett stayed too far away from me to even have a discussion, or for me to suggest we leave. I began to wonder why I'd visited him. What upset me most was Everett's complicity in the situation, as if he refused to be inconvenienced by my presence, that he would not alter his plans to accommodate his guest.

I knew to play the role, compliment his teammates, engage in a few dry quips and laugh at clever jokes. For the length of the party, which dragged on for more than two hours, I stole glances at the boys who seemed to be his closer friends, and wondered which one of them had taken that revealing Polaroid of him.

Finally, after some of the boys had retreated to their rooms, Everett gave me a tour of his own dorm. I had naively hoped to sleep there until being introduced to Randall, his studious roommate, who was not going anywhere.

Everett changed into track pants, a T-shirt, sweatshirt and a jacket, put a few items from a drawer into his pockets, then briefly retreated to the bathroom. My attempts at small talk with his nearly mute roommate crashed and burned.

"We're going for a walk," Everett announced upon returning. "I'm taking Reid to the guest dorm." The roommate nodded, said nothing.

"He's a charmer," I said as we strolled down the hallway.

"Randall Don't Call Me Randy? Yeah, he's really quiet. And smart. That's about it."

"I figured you'd room with someone more–"

"More like me? Hell, no. One alpha per room. It's much better."

"Like most primates?"

"Especially our branch of the family."

"So, I guess he's the reason I can't sleep over in your room. But can you stay in the guest dorm?"

Everett shook his head. "Sorry. The night staffer there's an old crank. I can go in with you for a while, but we have a curfew at eleven. We can go into town to a little diner in a while, if you like."

"Sure."

So, that was it? Thanks for visiting, let's have a cheeseburger, and goodnight?

"Anyway, big day, huh?" I said, hoping to refrain from complaining about not having any time alone with him. The early evening air was a bit damp. Crickets chirped somewhere.

"Yeah, it's cool. We win three more and we go to state."

"It was great to see you play."

"Thanks. I wanna see you next week, too; see you stride past the finish line first."

"Yeah, probably more like twenty-seventh."

"Come on." He led me down an unlit path towards a cluster of tall trees.

I explained my own calculations on my probable place in the race, based on the other guys in our district, my time rates and training schedule changes, until I realized he wasn't listening, so I shut up. We were in the woods. It was pretty.

With a conspiratorial grin and a secretive skulk to his pace, Everett led me a short distance off the school campus.

"And here we are." He had stopped walking, turned to face me, as if this were our destination.

"Where's … the dorm?"

"It'll keep." He approached me, pressing his lips to mine.

"Now?" I pulled away. I would have embraced the idea more, but the way he just sprung it on me was odd.

"Is there a problem?"

"No, I just …" I glanced around cautiously. "Ev, do you like getting caught?"

"No, Reid. Well, yes, maybe. But if I really wanted that, we could go to the gym showers."

"What?"

"Joke. Sort of." He drew close, pressing his palm to my chest. "I just thought you understood."

"Understood what?"

"There are so many things we can't do, places we can't be ourselves. Here," his upward glance drew me to the dark tree branches, oaks mostly, canopied above us, "God sees us and likes it."

Wrapping his arms around me, we kissed and dry-humped with a warm familiarity. I avoided a few of his newly-earned elbow scrapes.

"I get it. I just, I don't know this place. Is it safe?"

"You think I jack off in my room? With Randall in there?"

"Oh." Just as I thought of 'my' woods back home, this was his private place.

Embracing me again, he whispered in a corny seductive tone, "So, does my big Giraffe wanna?"

"Yes, 'Monkey,' he wants to."

"Good. You can keep watch."

He was right, and knelt before me to prove it. It was the perfect setting. While secluded, the distant campus lights offered just enough of a glow to see Everett's face bobbing at my groin. I stroked my fingers through his hair, tugged an earlobe, quietly humming approval, until he stood up and whispered, "I want you to fuck me."

He unceremoniously turned and dropped his pants. The stark sight of his curved butt cheeks as he arched his back and leaned against a thick tree trunk sent a surge of lust through me, but also confusion. He wanted to do it standing?

"Oh, wait." He dug for something in his jacket pocket. "Here." He handed me a small tube of KY.

I slathered a bit on my cock, then brought my hand to the fuzzy crevice between his legs. As my finger dug up inside him, he flexed his muscles with pleasure, reached back and pulled me closer. I aimed, pointing myself toward him, and into him. I pulled up his sweatshirt and jacket, licking up his back until he shucked them both off completely. His pale skin glowed in the dim light.

Cautiously glancing around at the darkened woods, I expected his teammates to pounce upon us in some mad hazing ritual. But no one stopped us.

The wind shushing through tree branches was our mood music. We began an awkward, then comfortable, back and forth thrusting. That fleeting surge of power over him, even given willingly, was as exciting as the night breeze against my skin.

I reached around to paw his chest, join him in stroking himself. I licked the nape of his neck while his hand held my thigh, gripping it harder. At one moment, a leaf fell from the tree, landing on his back and sticking to a trail of my spit. I slid in deeper, until he was almost sprawled against the tree. Shoving myself closer, I found my hand atop his as it gripped the trunk. Bark crumbled between our fingers.

We grunted and moaned and giggled and grabbed. As with our first time, the steam around us became visible, but this time it was more of a mysterious mist in the night. Overcome with pleasure, I almost burst out a cry of love for him. Nothing could pull us apart, until finally, sticky and satiated, we did, with a mutual regret.

"Did you happen to bring a wet towel?" I joked.

"Here," he said, offering his undershirt as a sort of rag.

We pulled our pants back up. I helped him untangle his sweatshirt and jacket, helped him dress. Everett grabbed the balled-up undershirt I had dropped. "A souvenir," he joked after wiping his butt. Feigning disgust, I nevertheless accepted it.

We sat down together, leaned against the trunk and nuzzled for a while, not needing to talk.

"Wasn't that worth the wait?"

I shook my head as I wiped my fingers again on his shirt. How could I explain that it wasn't just about the sex, that I'd begun to clutch a spare pillow at night, pretending to hold him, that even the occasional chirp of his voice when he spoke in a joking tone brought flutters of pleasure inside me?

But he was right. His company was always worth the wait.

After getting my backpack from the car and checking me into the guest dorm, Everett walked with me to the small downtown main street of Saltsburg, where we nearly had the diner to ourselves. We ate slowly, talking quietly of plans to be together for the few weeks between our graduation and my departure for the park job.

Through the meal, and our slow walk back to the campus in the night, I found myself admiring his ability to shift gears so swiftly. One minute we were passionately humping in the woods, and then we casually shared French fries in a restaurant. Yet he was able to keep that intimate connection with a mere glance or the briefest touch.

My restless night of sleep alone in a nearly empty wing of the small guest dormitory felt like a detention, until Everett arrived the next morning, chipper and casual, offering a good morning kiss before we left the dorm room.

Over a noisy breakfast in the crowded school cafeteria, a few of his classmates made innocuous jokes and offered earnest farewells.

Everett walked me around the campus. We kept the talk light, nothing too intimate. We enjoyed the brisk morning air while sharing admiring glances, but barely touched. Before long, Everett had gradually guided me to my dad's Pontiac in the parking lot.

I had hoped we could spend the rest of the day together, but he offered up a volley of impending duties in addition to homework. I was also behind in my own studies but would have ignored them just to spend more time with him.

As if to cheer me, he said, "Hey, I made something for you for your birthday."

"Really?"

"But it's not done yet. I'll mail it to you."

"You could just bring it when you visit next week."

"No, it's almost done. I'll mail it."

"Okay. What is it?"

"It's nothing, just ... Thank you for coming." He held a serious look, until it grew into a mischievous grin before he added, " ... up my butt!"

Our laughter bounced across the parking lot.

"So, we're cool, right?" he said as we settled down.

Actually, we weren't. Jealous of his schoolmates for their casual privilege of simply being with him every day, leaving him once again pained me. I couldn't hold him in my arms as we had when we'd slept over at

Holly's, and I wondered when that would ever happen again.

Yet I agreed. "We are extra cool."

Chapter 17

Days later, as I was scolding myself for harboring conflicted thoughts about Everett, the gift he mentioned arrived in the mail.

Inside a small cardboard box the size of a postcard was a cassette tape. I figured Everett had made a mix tape which included some of 'our songs,' and I was partially right.

Laying on my bed with my little cassette player and earphones, I listened. It sounded like he was taping songs from a nearby radio, starting with the Fleetwood Mac song that played when we had first made out, indoors, at least.

But Everett's voice came in, whisper-singing, making up accompanying lyrics that sometimes made no grammatical sense, but which told of that afternoon on his bed. He even mentioned the tree cookies.

Apparently he had a portable cassette recorder and separate radio, or had borrowed one, because the background noises fluctuated from what was probably his dorm room during a moment alone to some other room. A few of those had been interrupted by a door sound, some brief chatting.

But as the tape continued with abrupt stop-starts as segues, Everett found acoustically sound areas, and sang along to Cheap Trick's "Dream Police" in what he narrated, like some frazzled war reporter, "the lone hill overlooking the sad prison where a flock of young boys toil in the brain camps of their despotic ruler..."

His comic voice faltered at one point, and switched to another clicked stop/start. I could hear his mouth close to the microphone, whispering, like a voice in a dream, "Reid. I miss you so much it hurts. I wanna see you soon. I have a lacrosse game the day before your berfday. Then we're together again, okay?"

He broke into some made-up song, I thought (it was actually Genesis, he would later tell me), howling at the wind, which muffled the microphone and distorted his closing chorus. I knew this wasn't just some silly game for him. He was pouring his heart out into a tiny box for me.

Weeks later, after what would happen in just a few days, I would sneak into the living room in the near dark, insert the tape into my dad's stereo, which had a cassette-to-cassette copier along with the record player. I would make copy after copy of that precious recording. Because I knew, after listening to it again and again, that I would wear it out.

Chapter 18

A freak accident, they kept calling it.

As if getting intentionally whacked in the head with a wooden stick by an opponent was freakish, and not just part of the game.

This is how it was described to me.

At one point, oddly only minutes into the lacrosse match, Everett was soaring across the field, had caught the ball, jumped mid-air to catch it, when an opponent deliberately collided with him across the side of his waist. He fell to the ground sideways, mostly on his hip, and a portion of his spine went the wrong way.

That mid-air moment, imagined in my mind, repeated over and over again. Those two or three seconds lurched his life into a completely unforeseen and irrevocable direction.

At first, I didn't cry when Holly called me. I was too busy feeling like a complete louse.

Her call came two days after the accident. Not knowing his injury was the reason he hadn't shown up at the half-marathon or my birthday party, I only felt hurt and disappointed by his absence.

I had won fourteenth place in the race the day before and was going to celebrate with some beers in the garage with the guys. I had hoped to announce, upon his dependably stunning entrance, like a low-class debutante ball, Everett Forrester, my boyfriend.

And I knew none of them would have had a problem with it, which was why I wanted to do it.

Holly had tracked down my family's thankfully listed phone number and called on that cold quiet Monday afternoon, when Mom was over in one part of town while Dad was in the opposite. I was alone in the house, doing absolutely nothing except feeling angry, just fucking angry about Everett's absence, when Holly called and told me everything.

Sitting on the kitchen floor, dizzy, the room had begun to spin around. I needed to be lower, closer to the floor, to piece together the timing of events.

While I was anticipating the meet the next day, my little party, and what would have been my daring announcement, Everett was being flown by helicopter to a hospital in Pittsburgh.

While I was warming up that morning and feeling the good pain of stretching, Everett's pain was dulled by an IV hook-up of morphine.

While I was feeling the tear of oxygen and carbon dioxide coursing in and out of my lungs as I ran, Everett lay face down on an operating table as a surgeon sliced open the flesh above the intersection of his buttocks.

Slumped on the sofa as my parents handed their moping son his birthday presents, at the same time Everett's parents and sister listened in a waiting room as a surgeon offered hopeful condolences and grueling medical facts.

I had been pissed off at him while he was pissing into a tube.

I told Holly I wanted to run downtown and catch the next train to Pittsburgh to see him. But she reminded me that a lot of people ahead of me simply had to pay their respects in what Holly called "this orgy of sympathy." Most of them weren't allowed to see him yet.

"So, what's your address?" Holly asked me, oddly changing the topic from Everett's accident.

"Why?"

"The photos? The ones I took of you two?"

I had forgotten about them. Between the talk of visits and calming each other, hopes and panic, the unspoken thought between us was that I might be the last person to ever make love with Everett, and those photos were the testament.

Chapter 19

What I had initially considered a less than perfect romantic night with Everett –that night at his sister's apartment– would become my salvation over the next several weeks. Holly became my telephone informant, a go-between for updates on Everett's condition.

I didn't have the temerity to ask if, in the middle of it all, he'd mentioned me. But somewhere in her second or third call, after her work and hospital visits, she said, "He wanted to know if you got the tape he sent." I told her to tell him I did, and I loved it.

My mention of the newspaper article didn't surprise her, at first. The *Greensburg Tribune* featured a photo of an ambulance parked next to the school playing field, taken by some ambitious Pinecrest student photographer, and beside it, the smiling senior portrait of Everett. The headline read, 'Forrestville Teen in Sports Accident.'

"On the front page?" Holly said in disbelief.

"Well, not much happens around here, as you may recall."

"Damn. Slow news day," she added caustically.

Not knowing whether to suggest sending her the clipping, I also didn't say that I'd snuck out of the house to buy two more copies. Each night, I stared at the newspaper photos.

School became a ghost walk. Coasting on my eleven and a half years of good grades, I almost forgot about the senior college placement exams, until mimeographed pages of reminder schedules were doled out in class. Study? Why? Track practice continued. Training? Why bother?

Forcing myself through the habits of high school, for the next week I shifted books and objects from one place to another; cleats on, cleats off, pencils dulled, clothes discarded or not, as my body sat, walked, ran, then collapsed.

"Reid?"

A parent, I forget which one, wanted to have a talk.

"We know you're upset, but there's nothing you can do. We just have to hope for the best."

Platitudes over plates of food, consumed, digested and excreted. Flower arrangements and Get Well cards chosen, delivered. Television, records and silence, heard and ignored.

"Reid?"

And then, I got another call from Holly, late at night. She sounded a little drunk.

"They're going to do another operation, but he's probably paralyzed for life."

"How much?"

"It's, they said it's in the lumbar region, his lower back."

"That means he might–"

"They're not making any promises. He's probably... oh, Reid, it's so awful. He's gonna be on his stomach, just laying there, with stitches on his back for a few weeks. And they keep dragging him off for more X-rays, and he's got all these fucking tubes in his—"

"Is he conscious?"

"Yes."

"Can he talk?"

"Yes, yes. It's just slow-going right now."

"Okay."

She sounded exhausted. I stopped asking questions.

"But we're lucky."

"Lucky?"

"He didn't break his neck," Holly said. "It's what they call an incomplete injury. That means he might get some sensation below the injury. Because it was so low—"

"Lumbar," I recalled, like some strange new mantra.

"Right."

A pause, and Holly sighed, overwhelmed. I wanted to be strong. But instead, out it came, pleading, "I need to see him."

"I know. But you have to wait."

"I know." I didn't, actually.

Between sniffles and swears, Holly updated me on every detail she could think of. I listened to each aspect of his accident, tying and untying a corner of my T-shirt into and out of knots.

While my own parents would come to be clear in their defenses over the ensuing weeks, other people would prove to be barriers, and opposition sprang up from the least likely places.

Chapter 20

Why I Need New Glasses;
A Mandatory Essay Composed in My First,
and Hopefully Last, Detention Period
by Reid Conniff

Testosterone, a steroid hormone from the androgen group, is found in mammals, reptiles, birds and most vertebrates. In mammals, it is secreted in the testes of males and the ovaries of females. The male mammal produces ten times the amount of testosterone as females of the same species.

Testosterone in males plays a key role in the development of muscle mass, bones and body hair. Although, contrary to images portrayed in popular culture, when produced in excess, it can result in the loss of body hair, particularly on the head. Inconclusive studies have presumed that excess testosterone production, and possibly excessive masturbation, may lead to premature balding. This is contrary to anecdotal folklore regarding hair on palms, which is scientifically impossible, as the flesh of the palms of homo sapiens do not normally include hair follicles.

This essay will focus on male mammals, and show, by recent example, the hazards of its secretion in excess or conditions of stress.

Confrontation between male homo sapiens can often lead to a sudden production of adrenaline.

Adrenaline is a hormone secreted by the adrenal medulla after stimulation in the central nervous system in response to stress, anger, or fear.

It is my conjecture that the events which led to my detention are marked by excess production of a combination of testosterone and adrenaline on the part of one homo sapiens named Wendell Graff.

Following the news of the traumatic accident and subsequent hospitalization of a close friend, my performance as a member of our high school's track and field team's long distance individual event competitions became what can objectively be called sub-par.

This generally decreased the quality of my running form and my concluding time results. But at no time did our adult supervisor, the team coach of both Mr. Graff and myself, ever imply by word or action that I might consider removing myself from the competition roster.

Yet Mr. Graff, whose verbiage and remarks are regularly tinged with racist, homophobic and generally inane comments both on and off the field of competition, saw fit to make himself a representative, without consent, for the entire team, via negative critique of my performance. This occurred on several occasions, mostly at tournaments, but also in training sessions.

Mr. Graff, whose body type can accurately be described as an endomorph, or in the vernacular, husky, portly, or in crude form, fat, possesses limited experience in the athletic events to which I am more experienced, specifically, long endurance aerobic activity through running.

Mr. Graff, who is limited in his expertise in the field area of throwing objects, took it upon himself to share, aloud, in the company of fellow teammates, misinformed and inexperienced comments about my decrease in competitive skills. Graphic and monosyllabic terms used for female genitalia and homosexuals were the most common terms uttered.

It was upon the day in question when Mr. Graff offered up a puzzling conundrum.

Diverting his unsolicited critiques away from athletic skills, Mr. Graff called into question a previous private event involving myself and another person –not a student at this school– to which his opinion was neither relevant nor requested. I later learned that his information was gathered from a gossiping cousin of Mr. Graff who worked at the place where he had seen myself and the other person.

As an odd and irrelevant comparison, Mr. Graff noted my infrequency in the school's locker room and shower facility after training sessions as being worth questioning my masculinity.

It was at that point that I queried Mr. Graff, and I quote, "So, not wanting to see you naked makes me a fag?"

At that point, Mr. Graff, apparently at a loss for words, took to fisticuffs. My glasses were strewn from their place on my person and fell aside. Mr. Graff then hit me again, inducing my bloody nose, a mild non-concussive wound, which healed soon afterward.

It was then that our fellow teammates, specifically fellow senior Kevin Muir, intervened, and the physical aspects of the argument were halted, while loud words continued to be exchanged until our supervising coach intervened.

By using this incident as a personal example of a possible chemical imbalance of testosterone and adrenaline at the stressful moments described, it is my layman's opinion that Mr. Graff be asked to undergo drug testing, psychological counseling, and if needs be, expulsion from our fine learning institution.

Formal legal proceedings are unnecessary. However, financial compensation for a pair of replacement prescription glasses, amounting in the sum of $43, seems only fair.

Chapter 21

Packing a few things for my visit to Everett, I felt a change in my thoughts about him. My fear of him dissolved. My worries about his reckless nature, the way he used his charm, and my jealousy of it and his friends, all became pointless.

While both my parents had expressed an interest in joining me on my first visit to see Everett, they backed off when a flush of emotion overcame me. With few words, they understood the importance of my seeing Everett alone, and my insistence on taking the train to Pittsburgh. I didn't think I could manage driving.

Any visitor to Greensburg is quick to notice the Clock Tower. It's a point of pride for the locals, one of the many old-fashioned buildings that give the town its folksy charm. Less than charmed by having missed the train, I waited another half hour after Dad dropped me off.

In a gesture that I had hoped would lift Everett's spirits, I had purchased a small baby evergreen tree in a plastic pot and placed a tiny ribbon around the top branch.

The plant got more than a few glances from other passengers during the wait and through the hour on the train. I set it on the empty seat beside me while I tried to read one of my textbooks.

Distracted, I gazed out the window as Greensburg gradually changed to the outlying industrial areas, then a green blur of hundreds, then thousands, of trees. That so many of them continued to thrive despite development and wildfires gave me hope.

I asked a station attendant for the best route to the hospital. The city's convoluted bus route map confused me at first. But I figured out the one transfer, and finally found myself before an immense grey cement complex of buildings. Weaving around hospital workers, hallways and elevators, it took another twenty minutes to find the ward where Everett's room was.

Anxious to finally see him, to present my thoughtful gift to him, I ignored the low laughter I heard as I approached his room, thinking it was from some other patient's friend.

But seated with his feet up and crossed at the foot of Everett's bed was my track teammate and recent helpful defender, Kevin Muir.

"Hey, Conniff, my man!" Kevin greeted me as if I had merely strolled into a bar like a regular. "How's that left hook?"

Everett appeared relaxed, or gave the impression of nonchalance, as easily as an immobile hospital patient could. He looked pale and gaunt.

Stunned by this pairing, I stood still, the evergreen plant quivering in my hand.

"Aw, you brought me a little tree," Everett smiled, sharing what I hoped would be a secret gesture. His look assured me he understood.

"You just missed his mom a while back," Kevin said. "She probably would of chased you out with the broom she rode in on."

I stood in the doorway, completely flummoxed.

"We were just talking about you," Kevin said, casually.

Yes, casual was apparently the attitude I was expected to assume, despite the fact that I was perplexed by Kevin's presence, overwhelmed to see Everett, and fighting off the urge to clutch him in my arms and break down sobbing.

"Givin' Evey the blow by blow," Kevin grinned.

"I told Kev you were gonna stop by," Everett said, again, casually. But his glance revealed a silent command. Be cool.

"Huh."

"Come here."

I leaned in, gave Everett an awkward hug as he stole a brief kiss. I had hoped that his parents' having paid extra for a private room might provide a more intimate greeting.

"Ooh, shiner," Everett reached up. I shivered as his fingers grazed my face.

"Defending your honor, sir." I bowed ceremoniously.

"Thank you for that, and this," Everett said, holding the plant appreciatively, before he tried to place it on a side table. I took it from him and set it down.

I started to move back, but Everett's hand grabbed my arm, so I stood close. "So, how do you–"

"We been neighbors since we were kids," Kevin explained. "Used to play together all the time."

"Oh, right." I remembered my mentioning Kevin on our drive to Pittsburgh. Everett's dismissive tone at the time made me question their connection.

And then I understood more clearly. Despite Everett's private school years, they both lived in the wealthy neighborhood on the other side of the forest. Kevin had been his playmate. He got there first.

"Hey, innit a lil late for a Christmas tree?" Kevin asked.

"It's kind of a private joke," I said.

"Oh."

"It's a silver fir. Actually, most conifers retain their needles through the winter, thus the evergreen name." I was rambling, Kevin was oblivious, but Everett grinned.

With my anticipation of a private confession of love and devotion halted by Kevin's presence, I found a second chair and sat down by Everett's side. We shared some aimless talk about the track season and Kevin's slightly boastful tales of accomplishment with pole vault and 'the ladies.'

I kept my resentment mostly undetectable, repeating, "So, you guys know each other from when you were kids?"

"Yeah, for a while." Kevin's knowing nod and Everett's grin betrayed some secret shared history.

"Until..." Everett hinted.

"Until," Kevin echoed. "One Christmas, we were about twelve. I got Evey a BB gun. We weren't gonna kill anything with it, just shoot at tree trunks. We were always playing in the woods. Anyway, his mom came marching over, bangin' on our door, and she chewed out my parents like they were criminals, and shoved that gun into their hands. She officially declared us 'not friends' after that."

Actually, Kevin was somewhat entertaining, and Everett, still weakened by what he was enduring, listened amiably, though his dopey grin may have had more to do with his pain medications.

In the middle of an awkward pause where we had collectively run out of things to talk about, other than the obvious –Everett's probably being unable to walk for the rest of his life– and the unspoken –that Everett and I were somewhat secretly boyfriends– Kevin got up, saying he had to "hit the road."

"Hey, Kev, do me a favor," Everett said.

"Sure, Evey."

"Take my bro here out and get him high. Holly says ever since all this, he's been miserable."

For a few moments, they both laughed at me, I thought. But when I falsely joined in as some kind of defense mechanism, the embarrassment passed.

"Listen, I'm gonna head out." Kevin leaned over the bed, gave Everett a friendly hug, as much as was possible.

"Take care," he said to Everett. Then, as if a date had already been set, Kevin approached me with a manly pat on the shoulder. "Gimme a call tonight. You doin' anything?"

"I don't know when I'll be back home."

"Cool. Come on by any time. It's the white house, down the street from Evey's."

And with that, I was finally alone with Everett. I stood, exaggeratingly stunned.

"'Evey?' Did you call him Kevey?"

Everett shrugged it off. "I told you. We're old friends. I haven't seen him in years."

"You don't need to explain." The joyous tearful reunion I'd anticipated had been derailed.

"I want to explain," Everett argued. "You know him from school. I knew him when we were kids, and a little bit after that."

"So you..."

"What?"

"You know."

"It was just messing around."

I nodded.

"To him."

"He's like, with a different girl every year," I countered.

"Exactly."

"What does that mean?"

"Nothing is what it means. Come 'ere." He opened his arms.

I felt the rise of tears as I held him, nestled in the aroma of his medicinal-tinged sweat. His kiss to my neck led to my cheek, then lips, as I adjusted myself to face him. He held on, so I cautiously climbed onto the bed and lay beside him.

He reached a finger to dab at one of my tears, then brought it to his lips. "Now, that means something."

I slowly caressed his face. He closed his eyes, tingling at my touch, it seemed.

"Can you stay a while?" he murmured. Despite his gaunt complexion, he still retained a ghost of the near-simian charm I'd grown to adore.

"Sure. Last train back's at eleven."

"You took the train?"

"It was cool. My parents had stuff to do, so—"

"They'll kick you out at nine."

"Okay. We have a few hours."

"Ooh, baby," he taunted.

"Not for that. And not here."

"Well, just keep touching me," he whispered. "If you can stand it."

"That's why I'm here."

"And promise me?"

"What?"

"Hang out with Kev. He's a jerk, but he's a nice guy."

"I know."

I shared with Everett how Kevin had recruited me back to the track team, how I wasn't sure why he'd done it. Perhaps just being Everett's boyhood friend had had something to do with it.

"Besides," Everett said, "As I recall, he's hung like a donkey."

I gasped in false shock, but confirmed his comment by sharing the amusing sight of Kevin's revealing pole vaults.

"Well, you know what Holly says," Everett said.

I waited, confused.

"Be good. And if you can't be good…"

"…be perfectly wicked," I finished.

"Hey, you oughtta stay with Holly when you visit," Everett said. "She likes you. She can keep you posted on my schedule. I don't want you coming this far and have me stuck with doctors all day."

"Sure. Sounds like a plan," I answered, tabling my confusion. It felt wrong to grill him about Kevin. Was Everett trying to set me up with a sexual substitute? Was this a not-subtle hint that all things romantic between us were over? I was too confused to even question such an idea.

As we cuddled, Everett began to doze off, but then said softly, as if half asleep, "When I get better, we can take another nice romantic walk in the woods."

It pained me to lie to him, but I did. "Sure. It's a date."

I tried to slowly leave his side, but, half-awake, his arm pulled me back. We nuzzled, until a stern nurse announced the end of visiting hours.

Somehow, in the dark of that night, I kept myself composed. Finding my way around, up and down hills via buses, back to the train station, into a seat on another train, through those forests, tunneling through mountains, I returned home.

Only after reporting to my parents about Everett's condition over a wolfed-down reheated dinner, omitting references to Kevin and so many private moments, did I finally retreat to my room, where I clutched a pillow and silently cried myself to sleep.

Chapter 22

Despite the emotional drain of that first visit, I planned a regular schedule. The next Saturday, after a disappointing dual track meet where I placed fourth in the five-kilometer, I called Holly to check on his day. It was a good thing I did.

"He's all booked up today with doctors and therapists."

"Should I come anyway?"

"Sure, why not? You can stay over, then we can both visit on Sunday, too. The coast'll be clear."

By that, she meant her mother would not be visiting. At some point after his accident, Mrs. Forrester had heard about our little spring fling at the country club.

"Hey, bring a jacket and a tie. I can get you a ticket to the opera I'm working on."

"Which one is it?"

"*The Cunning Little Vixen.* It's about animals. You'll like it, even if you don't like opera. The designs are freakin' amazing, if I do say so myself. I have to work backstage. Those big-assed ladies and queens are always busting out of their costumes."

Perhaps her cheerful invitation was a way of compensating for the whole situation. While I didn't expect Holly to maintain a hand-wringing state of grief, it seemed a bit odd. But given our interactions before Everett's accident, I shook it off as Holly just being herself, getting on with life.

With a little extra packing, I made room for a jacket I borrowed from Dad, placing it carefully in a suit bag. I didn't want to borrow either of my parent's cars. I wanted to be without obligation.

Dad once again drove me to the Clock Tower train station downtown. I got out to buy a round-trip ticket, checked the time for the next train, and returned to Dad, who sat in his car waiting.

"You okay?"

"Sure."

"Need any money?"

"Mom took care of it."

"Okay. Look, Reid ..."

"Yeah?"

"I just ... Tell Everett we're sending good thoughts his way."

"Okay."

I knew he'd wanted to say more, perhaps ask me why I insisted on visiting Everett again. He'd probably realized while trying to form a hesitant protest or word of caution that it wouldn't matter what he said.

As I'd been warned, Everett's day was a full one. I waited patiently in a chair outside his empty room for about two hours, almost getting lost in a textbook, when one of the patients on a gurney being wheeled past me held out a hand.

"Jerr-affe," Everett half-sang. We brushed fingers as a nurse turned and pushed him into his room.

"Hey, Monkey." I stood.

"Oh, good," said the nurse, an older Asian woman. "You have a cold or any infectious diseases?"

"No, Ma'am."

"Good. You can help."

It took a little effort, but I figured out how to hold Everett, help him sit up and transfer from the gurney to his bed. The nurse asked Everett if he wanted me to leave the room as she adjusted his catheter.

"He's seen it before," he smirked through obvious exhaustion. Despite our familiarity, I did avert my eyes a moment after the nurse pulled back Everett's hospital gown. It felt wrong to be looking at his penis, even if he was my sort-of boyfriend. But I didn't know when, or if, I'd ever see him naked again, so it seemed slightly justified.

Finally satisfied with her work, the nurse left us alone.

"Hi."

"Hi."

"Holly says you're staying over. Cool."

"Yeah, it's ... You okay?"

"Oh, more poking and prodding. I think we're done with the hope for a miracle cure. But you never know."

It was late afternoon. A grey glow of refracted sunlight filled the room. Everett's haircut looked odd, as if he'd been shorn.

"Regeneration," I blurted.

"What?"

Some random science fact had popped into my head. "Nothing, I just ... Plants and trees can grow new branches even after they've been cut down, sometimes even after a fire."

"Okay," Everett replied warily. "So, I should think like a tree?"

"It couldn't hurt. I'm sorry. It's stupid. I'm just... I'm happy to see you."

"Well, good. 'Come forward, Scarecrow.'"

And I did, realizing I was standing awkwardly away from him. Delicately hugging him, I half-knelt while crouching beside his bed, as if about to offer a prayer. I found myself unable to find words.

Instead, we just held hands, which led to some aimless grazing of forearms. After a long while of serene silence, we two just looking at each other, Everett whispered out that little song.

"Every time I think of you, it always turns out good..."

The opera turned out to be quite entertaining, though stranger than I had expected. Written by Leos Janacek, and based on a comic book from the 1920s, it involved a female fox who becomes domesticated by a woodsman. The chorus included a lot of wildly costumed singers dressed as insects and frogs who were delightfully silly. But it was really about the fox. Unhappy being tied up in the woodsman's back yard, she breaks free. The fox is eventually killed, and a human bride later wears a coat with her pelt. In the final scene, the bereft woodsman returns to the forest where he first met the vixen.

As the audience poured out through the lobby, I waited for Holly as she had instructed, gazing up at the ornately decorated ceiling. I wanted Everett to be with me, to experience this. Looking at the doorways and staircases, I wondered how it would have been possible to even get him inside.

"So? What did you think?" Holly had arrived.

"Beautiful. Congratulations. Is that what you say to an assistant costume designer?"

"Yes," she said with an exhausted air. "Look at you, all preppy."

I blushed.

"So, let's get home and spark one. Pizza again?"

"Sure."

Since Holly had been the host of my first night spent with Everett, I felt a connection that dodged a clear definition. She had become a combination of sister, confidant and den mother for horny minors.

During the drive home in her car, her gossip about the backstage drama didn't dampen my admiration for the opera. She talked about the fussing before and even during the production, and the fascinating details of the construction of the animal and insect costumes.

We arrived at her apartment and began digging into the pizza we picked up on the way home. I sat down on the sofa bed where Everett and I had been so close, and felt yet another longing for him, as he probably lay sleeping or in pain on the other side of town.

Holly's offer of a beer and a bong hit didn't need a second invitation. Unlike that first night in her home, instead of zoning out, I found an ease in babbling about our shared concern, Everett.

"The sick thing is, our mom is secretly thrilled by all this." Holly toyed with the loose strands of her long hair, finally tying it in the back with a clip. "I mean, just when she's ready to let her kids go, you know, the empty nest thing, now all of a sudden she feels needed."

"Huh."

"I know. Freaky, right?"

"Yeah."

"She can't wait to get him home again. They're gonna release him in a few weeks. There's really nothing else to do, except teach him how to poop and exercise. Besides, the hospital bills are gonna tank my mom and dad, so she's hiring a private nurse."

"I didn't know."

"Yeah, we're not as rich as we look. At least not by next year, probably."

"Huh." I pondered that possibility. With Everett back in Greensburg, did I even want to take the state park job?

"You get along with your folks?" she asked.

"Oh, yeah, it's nothing like your– Sorry."

"No, don't be. They know about you?"

"They do now, thanks to your brother."

I leaned back on the sofa, as if resigned. Although she told me that Everett had shared our misadventures in some detail, I filled Holly in on my version of our recent encounter with her father.

"You should thank him."

"Who, your dad?"

"No, silly; Everett."

"Why do you think I'm here?"

"Because you love him?"

"Yes," I said, declaring myself so clearly again, despite being in an inebriated haze, or because of it.

"He's going to go through so much difficulty. I need to ask you. Do you ... Reid, do you really want to be here for all this?"

I considered Holly's blunt question, and thought about the opera, how perhaps Diana Forrester thought of me as nothing more than a fox in her henhouse.

"I really don't have a choice. I can't stop thinking about him; worrying, remembering what he did for me. I was ... I was this average guy last year, and he just set me loose. It's like, you know certain plants and flowers lay dormant for a season or more, until something or someone pries them open. I ... I owe him."

She pondered my response. "But is that love?"

"I don't know."

"I'm not– believe me, I am so on your side, and his side. But, you know, I had what I thought was love, and it took me all the way to Paris and back."

"Right." Behind me, the poster of that French painting loomed.

"It's funny," Holly said. "A few days after the accident, we were sitting in his room, Mom and I. Dad had been with us, but had to go back to work. Ev was all drugged up, and sort of half woke up, and said, 'My giraffe. Where's my giraffe?' Mom was so confused. She was like, 'He never had a toy giraffe. What is he talking about?' So I asked him about it days later, and he told me. It's you. You're his giraffe."

I don't know why I shoved the emotions back inside. I could have cried in front of her. I held them off, but Holly didn't.

"I call him Monkey sometimes. It's just ..."

I considered explaining to her that we'd come up with those nicknames while lying naked on her sofa. I didn't.

"You know he may never walk. He might never be able to–"

"That's not important."

"Yes, it is, Reid."

She was right. How would I be able to have any kind of relationship with Everett with a cluster of doctors and therapists and nurses, friends and protective parents always there?

"Are you still going to Temple?" Holly asked, as she blew her nose on a paper napkin.

"Yeah, and the park job for part of the summer, probably. But, I don't know. I filled out the admission forms and the scholarship application. But, I was thinking, maybe I could just take some classes at the Greensburg Penn State campus. I just ..."

"You should go. Philly's a big city. Maybe that'll give you some time to sow some wild oats."

"What do you mean by that?"

"It means, keep loving Ev, but don't lose your whole life over him. You're fuckin' seventeen."

"Eighteen."

"Oh. Happy Birthday, then." She handed me the bong.

The next day, at my insistence, Holly accompanied me to visit with Everett. I sat close to his bed, touching and holding hands for a while, since I was comfortable in her presence to do so. It was also relaxing to simply listen to their inside jokes and family stories. There were no awkward pauses, fewer longing glances, and I actually felt more comfortable.

The truth was, I had begun to consider whether I had to let him go, and if so, how to do that.

Chapter 23

Despite their suggestions, I wasn't wicked. I didn't return Kevin's phone call a few days later. I waited.

Dad pestered me when I cancelled a planned visit to Temple University. He had the long drive all planned out. I told him I was just going to apply sight unseen, although I was still unsure. I couldn't pass up a weekend when I wanted to see Everett.

My two subsequent Saturday hospital visits became a regular pattern, until Everett said that he would be brought home. When he called on a Tuesday night, telling me he had finally been moved home the day before, I almost dropped the phone to run and see him. But he warned me.

"You have to be careful," he said, his voice soft. "My mom's not leaving the house much, and Helen's swooping down on the hour, plus I have this, ow, nurse."

I heard a noise, Everett attempting to adjust himself in what I assumed was his bed.

"Where are you?"

"Mom's got Dad's old office converted with this heinous hospital bed. Ergh. Hold on."

The phone thudded. I heard more grunts and fabric shifting, almost sensing his discomfort.

"You ready for a little cat burgling?"

"What?"

"Well, I'd let you in the kitchen door some late night, but I'm a tad indisposed."

"I'm sorry."

"What are you sorry for? It's not your fault."

"Ev, I'm–"

"Stop it."

"I was just going to say I'm confused. You want me to sneak into your house?"

"Why not? Daytime's better. Can you get out of school tomorrow? Helen's gonna be out shopping, and Mother's got some meeting with the club. Weekends they're all over me. The relatives have just been crawling out of the woodwork."

"You want me to–"

"Yes, brainiac. I want you to sacrifice an afternoon of abiding among the lower creatures at your inferior learning institution, make up an excuse, and come visit me, alone."

The plan was simple, or so I was told. First, check for cars. If the kitchen door was locked, Everett told me to try the back garage door. If that failed, he was going to ask that a window in the converted office be opened just a crack. He would complain of his new room being stuffy. Friday afternoons were his nurse's day off. Provided both Mrs. Forrester and Helen were out, as Everett promised, I would have three options for my little crime of permitted breaking and entering.

Getting out of school was almost too easy. I lied to my fifth period U.S. History teacher about having a headache, and on the way to the nurse's office, ducked into the boy's room and patted my forehead with some hot water. While her thermometer revealed no anomalies, I made a valiant effort of acting dizzy, and the indifferent nurse gave me a note to take to the principal's office, whereupon I was told I could either walk the three blocks home or await my mother's return call.

A gray rain spattered down over the parking lot. My walk across it left me uneasy. Why hadn't I pulled a stunt like this before? Perhaps because I had no reason, no one like Everett to inspire me.

I could deal with my mother's confusion later and either confess my activities or continue to feign some vague illness. Turning past the block that led to the strip of forest, I stepped through the woods and the muddy remnants of the recent downpour, until I once again walked along the street to his stately home.

Trying to appear nonchalant in his neighborhood, with a clear sense of purpose, I warily glanced around for any neighbors. Thankfully, there were none, and the back kitchen door was open. I spied a window slightly opened, but would have had to find some sort of footstool to reach it and make such a dramatic entrance.

The counter top and kitchen table were spotless. Helen must have been out. My boots were coated in mud, so I quickly removed them, leaving them on the porch.

Classical music played softly in a nearby room. I walked toward it, through the living room where delicate vases, objects and family portraits sat on tables and mantles.

In the office, a white-sheeted hospital bed with a metal frame held Everett's frail body. His eyes were closed. He seemed to be sleeping, despite the music, until I approached.

What had once been his father's office, with traditional dark green walls and wooden wainscoting, had been converted into a makeshift bedroom. Stripped of its previous furniture except a few chairs, a table was stacked with small boxes of medical supplies. Posters I recognized from Everett's room had been tacked up on the walls in a hasty effort at familiarity.

Beside the window, on a small table, the tiny evergreen tree I'd given him sat, almost forlorn, as if aching for its kin outside.

"My hero!" Although a bit groggy, Everett reached out his arms. We hugged, and I held him, cautious not to squeeze too hard.

"Oh, it's so good to see you."

"You, too." I smiled. "How are you?"

"*Cogito, ergo doleo.*"

"Which translates to …"

"I think, therefore I'm depressed."

"I'm sorry."

"I missed you so much," he said, refusing to let me go.

"It's only been a week." I held his gaze. He looked pale in some places, and flushed with a fever or a rash in others. His arms lost their tight grip, but held on.

"Do I get a kiss?"

"Oh," I mumbled, and leaned in. He didn't taste quite right, and his mouth was dry. But we kissed, and my desire stirred, cautiously, as if it were unsure how to express itself to him.

In the hospital, I'd touched him so delicately, but here in private, his upper mobility having returned a bit, I felt him reach under my coat for skin, and we continued kissing, me bent over. I resisted, then felt his hand guiding me toward him, under a T-shirt, under the sheet, his warm stomach rising and falling with his breath.

"We gotta be quick."

"With what?"

"Whadda ya think? Drop 'em, sport."

"Here?"

"Why not?"

"But you're–"

"Paralyzed? Probably for the rest of my life?"

"I didn't mean–"

"Well, I did. I said it, okay?"

"Ev, I–"

"Don't start crying. I've been faking taking those damn pain pills for days so I could actually feel something, just waiting for you. Nobody's touched me at all, except to wipe my ass or poke needles in me. I need you."

His hand insistently grabbed for my crotch. Shocked, and a little turned on by the now familiar furtive nature of the situation, I relented.

There would be plenty of time for simple caresses and longing glances. But right then, like that urgent moment when we'd first met, I simply wanted him, and he seemed determined to defy any impossibility.

My reach downward between Everett's legs was brushed away. "It doesn't know what it's doing. Besides, if I take the tube out, I'll piss all over."

Everett's face looked suddenly flushed; his breathing had become a series of short pants, like an exhausted dog.

"What do you mean? Can you—?"

"Sort of. Not yet. Just ... damn fuckin' headache ..."

With another insistent grab, my belt open, my pants shucked down to my knees, I sidled closer to the bed, leaning in as Everett enveloped his lips around my erection.

"Mmm. I missed this."

For a moment, I had to close my eyes and pretend it was the old Everett, the whole Everett. I felt guilty, but it wasn't as if I was mentally cheating on him.

I thrust closer, allowing him easier access. He grabbed my balls with one hand, cupping a butt cheek with his other, pushing me closer. The cold metal bed frame banged against my knees.

"What if we just—"

His mouth full, he grunted disagreement, yanking my dick closer. I pushed my hips forward as he slurped with a determined hunger.

But still, the confusion and impulses of pure lust combined in a strange way. The music continued, too loud for us to hear the car, the door, and the footsteps.

That time, it was Diana Forrester who got an eyeful of my ass thrusting into the face of her son.

Chapter 24

At least I hadn't brought a BB gun.

I stewed silently as Diana Forrester demanded that I remind her of my home address and when the soonest possible time would be to "have a serious talk" with my parents, to lecture them on "morals."

The image of her storming the home of Kevin Muir, as in his tale, had clouded my mind as I pulled up my pants. She was enacting the same outrage, the same pattern of "protecting" her son from bad influences; he, the tempter, who had convinced me to skip school, enter their home like a thief, all for a quick blow job. He, the boy who connived my parents into letting me drive into Pittsburgh for drug deals and museum debauchery. He, the victim.

Shouting me out toward her front door, despite Everett's profanity-laden protests from his room, and my stuttered pleading that I retain my boots at the opposite kitchen door, Mrs. Forrester confusedly re-aimed her vitriol while leading me through the kitchen, assuring me that she would be "paying a visit" to my home within the hour.

I had to be fast.

Running was my strong suit, just not in mud-clotted boots, a wet parka, and a case of blue balls.

When I clomped into the house through the garage, Mom was in the middle of what appeared to be re-arranging the living room furniture as one of her old

Tom Jones albums blasted away on the stereo. A vacuum cleaner stood alone in the middle of it all.

"You might want to put everything back," I said as I turned down the stereo volume.

"Why?"

"We're expecting a visitor."

"Who?"

"Everett's mother."

"What for?"

"A lecture, I guess."

"What happened? Why aren't you in school?"

I hadn't even removed my coat, just the boots. Something about staring down at my socked feet made me feel stupid.

Having already done the whole coming out talk, at least via Dad, it rolled out in a burst. I explained how Everett had called, begged me to sneak in and visit him, and one thing led to another, and we had been caught.

"Again?"

"Well, it wasn't like it was in public or anything."

"Paralyzed or not, your little friend's a bit odd."

"Mom!"

"Aren't there any normal boys at school for you?"

We hastily replaced the chairs and sofa to a semblance of their original positions. We sat silently, waiting, until my mother sighed, "This is absurd," and left for the kitchen to prepare dinner.

Eventually, a Mercedes-Benz rolled up the driveway.

The moment Mom opened the door, Mrs. Forrester stormed in, peeled off her coat, as if she expected my mother to take it, which she did, then parked herself down on the sofa and started off with a fuming speech.

By the time my mom had calmed her down enough to quiet her repeated threats of "pressing charges," I began to wish I had brought a BB gun.

"I mean, your son was dripping wet. Everett could have caught pneumonia!"

"Germs aren't carried through precipitation," I muttered.

They both stared at me.

"Well, they're not."

Mrs. Forrester turned her piercing gaze to my mother. "Have you ever heard of a term called autonomic dysreflexia?"

"No," my mom replied.

I shook my head.

"It's a very serious condition for people with spinal cord injuries. Over-stimulation of any kind, particularly that which you ..." Mrs. Forrester rolled her eyes in disgust. "The symptoms are high blood pressure, headaches and, the point is, it can be life-threatening. Your son could have given him a stroke!"

Stunned, I didn't know what to say, but I was determined to do some research as soon as possible and find out if Mrs. Forrester was right.

"I need your assurance that this will never happen again," she insisted, as if those were the new lowered, non-litigious terms of the treaty.

"That what won't happen again?" My mother's confusion seemed genuine.

"This!" She tossed off a gesture toward me. "This ... lechery."

"You really think my son was completely responsible for this."

"Well, what else could—"

"You know, my son— I'm sorry, Reid, but I'm going to be blunt here— my son didn't start acting funny until he met your son. It's too bad you haven't noticed, but they've been dating for, well, pretty much all year. Everett and he send letters and talk on the phone all the time. They enjoy each other's company, and I don't see how Everett's accident should—"

"Are you supposing that—"

"I'm not supposing," my mother cut in. "I'm observing. I haven't seen my son this happy in years. What if they ... cooled things off and promised not to be so ... active."

If I thought getting caught mid-sex twice with Everett was embarrassing enough, this topped it by a long shot; our mothers discussing our sexual activity like two angry pet owners in a dog park.

I'd lost track of the argument, my ears clouded over by remembering the sight of Everett's face flushing, his breath shortening, thinking a mere act of fellatio could be fatal.

"Well, this is exactly what I mean," Mrs. Forrester said.

"What do you mean?" And then that sigh of my mom's told me that she had really had enough. This was the reason for those years of sarcastic casseroles. This was the reason she had so few friends. This was the reason, a few years earlier, that she laughed the entire time we all went to see *The Stepford Wives*.

"I'm not blaming anyone," my mother said, calmly. "I'm just sorry that you can't see what is so obviously a good thing."

Diana Forrester's mouth fell open in an overly dramatic pause. She stood to leave.

"Just ... keep your son away from mine."

"Actually, Diana, he's eighteen, and so is yours, right?"

"So?"

"So, they're both adults now, legally speaking, whether we like it or not."

"This is preposterous."

"No, what's preposterous is your son having to show you what he is, and so clearly, in order to maybe knock some sense into you."

Another gasp, and Diana Forrester let herself out.

My mother stood, her back to me for a moment, looking at the door that had just been slammed.

She then turned to me. "So, your little date didn't go very well."

"Nope." I was a bit stunned.

"Are we going to tell your father?" she asked.

"Is she going to tell him?"

"Something tells me she's not done with her little hissy fit."

"So, we have to tell him."

"Our way."

"Okay."

"Why don't you help me with dinner?" She led me into the kitchen. "Oh, and you're grounded."

"But, what was all that?"

"That was between me and her. Or, she and I. You," she plopped down a bag of raw carrots, "are grounded for leaving school and lying about it."

As I peeled carrots into playful shapes for a new-old recipe, my mother appeared to have overcome her dressing-down from the town scion.

"You've read a few Shakespeare plays, yes?" Mom asked.

"In school, yeah. Why?"

"Let's not let this get out of hand and end like one of those, mm-kay?"

"Verily."

We never heard another word from Everett's mother. She must have yanked his phone right out of the wall, because I didn't hear from him, either.

Chapter 25

It was the two bong hits.

It was the new Pink Floyd album.

It was the fact that, with his parents and two brothers conveniently not home, Kevin preferred to lounge around in shorts, in freeball mode.

It was knowing Everett had basically played pimp for the two of us. His being just down the street, even if bedridden and drugged up, provided an aphrodisiac by proximity.

It was the occasional sealed letter from Everett, infrequently given to me at school by Kevin or slipped into my locker, that both wound up my sense of hope and dashed it into despair. Passing me in the hall, Kevin's brief shake 'No' meant there was no note or word from him, or that Kevin hadn't even bothered to see him.

I was horny, and I could tell someone about Everett, about my love for him, about my fears for him, even to an apparently bisexual stud whom I'd never thought considered me as anything but another guy on his track team.

But my mouth would spend less time talking, and more time doing what Kevin wanted done to him, or more specifically, what one large, blood-engorged body part wanted done.

Afterward, he had complimented me for having a great deal more expertise and enthusiasm than most of the girls he dated.

Kevin would call, and I'd walk over to his house through the woods when his family was out, at least once a weekend night. He'd hint about sex, had even shown me a porn video, a straight one. His shorts would tent as his dick thickened, or, as with his pole vaulting, peeked out one way or another. What we did, or rather, what I did to him, left me feeling like less of a sexual partner and more of a human handkerchief.

It was disappointing to discover that sex without love, no matter how much better equipped that other partner was, could still be enjoyable, but not as much, not by a long shot.

Which was why, for reasons I didn't need to explain to Kevin, after a few weeks I declined his subsequent invitations to "hang out."

Somewhere in the midst of all this, during a pleading phone call to Holly that I be forgiven, even though I didn't see any need to apologize, she reminded me that any diplomatic efforts toward her mother had fallen on rather unsympathetic ears. She also explained that Everett wasn't in any position to defy her, either.

"So, ya got caught *infragrante el delecto*," Kevin mused as he extracted a small bag of pot from his Camaro's glove compartment.

I refrained from correcting Kevin's terminology. I had also refrained from sucking on anything of his other than the joints he'd rolled over the past few weeks. My own refusal, despite Kevin's large talents, puzzled him at first. Aspiring for monogamy seemed stranger than mere homosexuality. His reaction was similar to his casual attitude during our trysts. "Whatever."

Kevin had invited me to join him for a drive and a smoke before the graduation ceremony. I'd excused myself from my parents' company with the ruse of a small party beforehand, not revealing that the party consisted of Kevin, myself, and his stash.

Tightening the papers with a twist, Kevin grabbed his lighter, opened his car door, and nodded for me to join him outside to sit on the hood. He'd never smoked inside his "baby," as he called the Camaro. He'd trained me in the intricacies of discreet pot-smoking, which included always bringing breath mints and eye drops.

As we shared hits, the late morning sun glinted off his car window. He'd parked on a small back road in a rural section of town less than a mile from the school. Our graduation gowns and caps lay in plastic bags on his car's back seat.

"Great that you got that summer job," he said.

"Yeah," I replied, thinking of it as more of a scenic exile.

"I should come visit you, go camping. Ain't been up there in years. Last time was with Cheryl."

Cheryl was, Kevin confessed to me without much encouragement, my top competition for Most Talented in pleasing his desires for passive fellatio. I'd never met her. He'd showed me a wallet-sized yearbook portrait.

Despite our mutual closeness with Everett, I was using Kevin as much as he was using me. With him, I pretended to forget that the reason I succumbed to our casual sex was to try to forget Everett, the pain of being so close to him yet forbidden to see him.

Perhaps Kevin knew that. He proved it at that moment.

"So, you still ain't been to see Evey?"

"No. I told you. Getting caught 'molesting' their son has made his parents a bit wary of me."

"Yeah, well, she's a bitch; always was. She just wants to keep him locked up in that house like, like…"

"Miss Havisham."

It wasn't an exact analogy, but since I knew every high school student had been required to read it, some image of the forlorn Dickensian woman might be familiar to Kevin.

"Who?"

"The old lady in the British book you probably didn't read, with the dusty wedding cake."

"Oh, yeah. It's like her, but a guy."

I nodded agreement, handed him back the joint. He sucked in the last of it, and in his smoky breath-held-in voice, said, "Shotgun," nonchalantly aimed his puckered lips at me, and exhaled. I sucked it in, held it, and for the first time, as the smoke exuded slowly through my nose, Kevin kissed me.

He smiled, watching the last wisps of smoke escape.

"Man, you really hold that in."

"Cross country training. Lung capacity." I glanced at the noticeably increased bulge in Kevin's pants.

"You wanna…?"

"We're gonna be late," I said.

Reaching for the bottle of eye drops as we sat back in
the car, feeling that familiar rumbling in my bowels, I
added, "Besides, I gotta see a drag queen."

"Huh?"

"Paris Talsis."

"Who?"

After fast-walking with me to the school rest room,
Kevin had said something that stuck in my mind
throughout the ceremony, with all its speeches by
faculty and valedictorians who hadn't had to prove their
valor by defending the good name of their crippled
boyfriends.

Kevin had an idea. After getting stoned, his great
ideas usually floated away with the haze of smoke. But
this one stuck.

From the other side of the stall as he held my cap
and gown, Kevin had said, "Ya gotta find a way to get
him outta that house, man."

"How? Kidnap him?"

"No, somethin'… somethin' with a reason, like, one
that's far away from her."

I should have thanked Wendell Graff. If not for our
little altercation, and perhaps one-tenth percentage
point more in my GPA, I would have been one of the
capped and gowned students given the duty of making a
speech at our graduation ceremony.

As I half-listened to amplified words about "our
future," "our achievements" and "our legacy," as I
offered a hazy smile to my parents, seated up in the
bleachers of the gymnasium, to the moment later on

where my entire row of alphabetically-seated fellow students rose to accept their diplomas, as those square tasseled caps were flung up in the air, before they came flopping down to the gym floor, I realized what I needed to do about my future, about Everett's future, about our future.

Chapter 26

'Autonomic Dysreflexia is usually caused when a painful stimulus occurs below the level of spinal cord injury. The stimulus is then mediated through the Central Nervous System (CNS) and the Peripheral Nervous System (PNS). The CNS is made up of the spinal cord and brain, which control voluntary acts and end organs via their respective nerves. The PNS is made up from 12 pairs of cranial nerves, spinal nerves and peripheral nerves. The PNS also is divided into the somatic nervous system and the autonomic nervous system. The autonomic nervous system is responsible for the signs and symptoms of autonomic dysreflexia. The autonomic nervous system normally maintains body homeostasis via its two branches, the parasympathetic autonomic nervous system (PANS) and the sympathetic autonomic nervous system (SANS). These branches have complementary roles through a negative-feedback system; that is, when one branch is stimulated, the other branch is suppressed.'

Despite distance, maternal barriers and even the possibility of life-threatening make-out sessions, I dedicated myself to somehow being in Everett's life again.

I could not sleep with him each night, or any night, perhaps, even though my every night was full of thoughts about him. But that didn't mean I couldn't help him.

Being raised by two parents who nurtured my sometimes obsessive studying habits, when I said, despite having just graduated from high school, that I was going to the public library, I expected and received no questions until my return.

"What were you studying?" my dad asked as I walked up the driveway. He was in the garage with the door open, toying with the wires attached to a pair of old speakers he'd bought at a garage sale. "Getting a jump on your summer job?"

"No, spinal injuries." I extracted a thick pile of books from my backpack. I'd also taken notes from a few reference books and emptied a pocket full of nickels at the copy machine to save extensive medical charts.

Dad set a speaker down on his work table. "This is about Everett."

"Well, yeah."

Dad sort of sighed, as if he were rehearsing the words in his head. "I know you're … you have feelings for your friend, and that's fine. But, you have to consider what his family's going through. Now, I don't know if what his mother said was right or not–"

"That's what I want to find out."

"Fine. But the point is, I thought we agreed it's pretty clear that it might be a good idea to give him some space; give it some time."

"I just went to the library, Dad. I didn't go to his house. I haven't called him."

"Okay, but–"

"I'm taking that park job, even though you know I want to stay here."

"Yes, and we're very happy for you. I think it'll be a great opportunity."

"So, we're good. I'm behaving, right?"

"Reid."

"I'll be in my room."

Despite the fact that it should have been clear to any alert parent that Kevin was more of a bad influence to any boy than I was, since Everett's accident, he had regained visiting privileges to the Forrester home. Getting the information from Everett was easy enough, and sharing it with me a few hours later only furthered my resolve.

Satisfied with the spinal cord research I'd found, I shifted to an additional topic; poring over out-of-town phone books, state maps, medical journals, financial reports and periodicals. Research was my turf, and in that area, I was a hotshot.

Driving off with my mother's car on another half-lie was the least of my problems.

My parents had saved enough to help pay for the non-scholarship-funded portion of my tuition, and I'd been presented with a card and a check for $500, for college expenses, Dad had clarified.

But when I expressed an interest in buying some camping equipment, they were confused.

"Aren't you going to be living in a building?" Mom asked as we finished a non-whimsical stew. Mom had gotten a bit serious, worried. I did my best to recall some semblance of Everett's charm over that special dinner those few months back.

"Well, yes, but there'll be camping trips, and I'll have time off and want to explore. And that old sleeping bag is kind of moldy. You don't want me to be unprotected out there, do you?"

That clinched it. After claiming my intent to take the train into the city, despite the inevitable cumbersome packages of equipment, I was allowed to drive to Pittsburgh, which, I assured them, was the location of the best-equipped sporting goods store in the area.

What I didn't tell them was that it was also less than a mile from the home of Everett's father.

Chapter 27

Its emptiness puzzled me, but entering Mr. Forrester's nearly bare condominium in the downtown section of Pittsburgh proved once again that I should have put aside any expectations about Everett's disconnected family.

I didn't want to get Holly involved, so I didn't even tell her I'd be visiting. The possibility of both of us ganging up on her father didn't feel right. I would tell her later and knew she would eventually understand.

After a short awkward phone conversation telling him I would be in town for only that afternoon, Mr. Forrester agreed to meet with me and gave me his home address.

Inviting me in and getting me a soda and himself a beer, which I declined, he sat near me in a chair as I sat on a long black leather couch. The floor-length windows displayed an expansive view of the city.

On one nearly bare shelf I noticed a few framed photos of a smiling Mr. Forrester with younger versions of Everett and Holly, and another few of him with a different woman; younger, blond and definitely not his ex-wife.

There being so little to look at, I faced him when he said, "So, you're Everett's ... boyfriend."

He didn't seem to have a problem with that prospect, and already knew, but was learning a new term, at least with respect to his son.

His perplexed demeanor matched my own. I hadn't really got a close look at Everett's father at the Spring Fling, at least in daylight. Before me sat a taller, older nearly identical version of Everett. I would have thought that this would be how Everett would look in a few decades, were he able-bodied. And yet, there was something missing. That spark, the mirthful light I'd seen in Everett's eyes, was absent.

Boyfriend? I raced through my few months since meeting Everett. We'd never actually had what could be called a normal date. But there I was, hoping to save his life. "Yeah. I guess so."

"You know, you don't have to apologize for the, uh, incident at the club," he smirked. "Matter of fact, I thought it was kinda funny."

"Right. Well, his mother, your, uh, ex—"

"Diana is very protective of Everett."

"You never said anything about seeing us—"

"No."

"Well, it got out." Maybe Everett wasn't lying that time.

"Why would I?" his father asked. "I know Everett. I knew since he was little. He …"

"He what?"

"He announced at dinner one night that he wanted to marry his friend."

"Kevin?"

"I think that's the one."

"Everett said Kevin gave him a BB gun for Christmas, and—"

"Oh, jeez, I almost forgot about that. Yeah, she wasn't upset about the gun. That wasn't it at all."

"Oh, okay."

"That was just one of so many reasons we divorced. I
… I was upset and sad about Everett, and the way she
treated Holly, and lots of other things you don't need to
know about. But then, I just let it go. It took her a long
time to get over it. Maybe she never did. No, I don't
think she ever will."

"But your … Diana just blew a gasket."

"She still thinks of Everett as a boy. Now, Holly;
well, she's her own woman now, but–"

"Yeah, we've hung out. I like her a lot."

"Oh?"

I explained our visit, my subsequent stays at her
apartment, omitting the drug deal, museum sex, and my
night spent in the arms of his son, realizing he'd
probably figured out the last part on his own.

"I wanted to talk about your ex, his mom's
protective–"

"Hovering–"

"Yes."

"She won't let you see him."

"Pretty much."

"You know, the way she went on about you, after
this last time you got caught, I had some funny thoughts
about you."

"I'm sorry about that."

"I was joking."

"Okay." I extracted a large envelope from my
backpack. "I didn't see any way to bring this up with
her, because of all that. Mr. Forrester–"

"Call me Carl."

"Carl." It didn't feel right. "What she said, about autonomic dysreflexia ..."

"About what?" he asked.

"It's a condition spinal cord injuries, people with them, sometimes suffer when they get, uh, over-stimulated."

"Oh, that. I forgot what she called it."

"Yeah, well, I didn't. Scientific terms stick in my head until I figure them out. And, you know where Everett's injury is?"

"I paid for the X-rays."

"So you know it's low on his spine, the lumbar region."

"L-four, they kept saying."

"Right, well, while dysreflexia can often occur in thoracic spinal cord injuries, it's not as common for lumbar injuries."

"So, you're bringing a case for the right to ... make out with my son with scientific evidence?"

"No, I ... Yes, sort of."

"Well, that's certainly a bit more dry than that jerk who asked for Holly's hand in marriage a few years ago."

"Excuse me?"

"Nothing. I'm sorry."

I gripped the envelope in my hands. "Everett told me about how you, I guess, provided for the conversion of a downstairs room for him."

"She put the den furniture in storage, which I'm paying for. Guess I ought to ship it here, but–" He glanced around his home, as if considering that thought.

"I'm sure she wants what's best for Everett. We all do. But I did some research, and don't take this the wrong way–"

"Please. She's taken everything I've done for past five years the wrong way, right to the bank."

"I'm sorry about that."

"Whaddaya got?" He glanced at the envelope. "Incriminating photos?"

"No, sir." I grabbed the soda, gulped it down.

"Calm down. Look, we've been getting a vague prognosis from his doctors for two months. He might heal, he might not. It's exhausting, and we're not deluded. We're being realistic, but we're not giving up hope."

"Sorry. Yes. Here. I think this will help."

He took it, extracted a cluster of brochures. A few fell to the floor, which he retrieved, then splayed across the glass coffee table before us.

"As much as your ex-wife feels she can care for Everett, and as much as I want to see him, to be with him, I did some research and I found several facilities that, um, I think, could really help him."

"Diana said the nurse and Helen were doing that for now. We were planning on a rehabilitation regimen–"

"Yes, but them doing it with him alone; it's just... These places, there's one that's nearby, but the one, unfortunately, that's best isn't, but it has the most going for it. They have dorms or rooms made for– to help people get used to being independent and activities and the best–"

"You did all this yourself," he said, calming me, as I'd gotten a little worked up.

"Yes, sir."

"For Everett."

"Yes, sir."

"And you'd be okay if he were further away."

"Well, my mom does let me use her car every now and then, and she and my dad are pretty cool about, well, a lot more cool than your–"

"And this would get him away from Diana."

"I would be lying if I said I didn't have some self-interest."

"Are you always this formal?"

"Excuse me?"

Mr. Forrester, Carl, took a few long sips of his beer, set the glass down, and pored over the brochures. "I think we'll pass on Wilkes-Barre... Let's see... Altoona? These are not cheap."

"No, sir. But I think you know he's worth it."

"Hmm, what about this one here in Pittsburgh?"

"It's smaller, more expensive, just because of the location, I guess."

"You really wanna drive to Altoona? 'Cause I sure don't. The best thing is that we get to visit him, right?"

"Right."

"If we chose the University of Pittsburgh facility, he'd be right near downtown. He could really use that, doncha think? Us all being close by."

Actually, by September, I would be hundreds of miles away at college. "He ..." and then I choked up, exactly what I'd told myself not to do. "He can't ... you can't, she can't just drug him up and pretend he's never gonna get better."

"You know he may never walk again."

"I know that. I mean ..." I wiped my eyes. "He's still that wild funny smartass, somewhere inside."

"Just not now."

"I mean, you know him better than I do."

"I used to," he sighed, looking away, as if trying to remember something. "You wanna hear a funny story? Actually, it's not very funny. Matter of fact, it's downright corny. His mother? Well, her mother warned her about me, still says it, like some kind of 'I told you so.' She thought Diana was fooled by me, that I was nothing but trouble, that she 'couldn't see the Forrester for the trees.'"

"That is corny."

"Yeah, well, it's better than the usual apple-falling bullshit I got as a kid."

He paused, and I guessed that this was what older men did, commiserate. I realized that I was giving him the advantage over his ex-wife, geographically and financially.

"You love him, right?"

"He ... sir, Carl. My life completely changed since I met him. I have a job this summer. I'm not even going to be able to see him, probably, but I'd quit it if I knew I could see him really recover, no matter what that means. I'm not giving up on him. And I hope you won't either."

He sat back in the chair, taking me in, this bespectacled nerd who was basically telling him what to do for his own child.

And then I saw that long-gone spark light up.

"Have you eaten?"

"Um, not recently."

"Chinese or Mexican?"

"Either's fine."

"Good. Both." He rose swiftly, rooted around in a drawer in his kitchen, extracted a cluster of take-out menus, made two phone calls, and as we awaited the pair of deliveries, he almost demanded I have a beer with his second, so I relented.

Over our shrimp fried rice, pot stickers and tacos, I listened as Carl told me one funny story after another about the boy we both loved for completely different reasons.

Hours later, slightly buzzed and full of deliciously greasy food, I shook Carl's hand, then drove out to a sporting goods store and bought myself a few hundred dollars worth of camping supplies.

Chapter 28

Dressed in a black windbreaker and ski cap while carrying a footstool, it would have been rather difficult to explain myself to anyone who discovered me skulking through the woods to the back of Everett's house. Fortunately, no one did.

Knowing a tossed pebble wouldn't do any good, since he couldn't come to the window, and the possibility of getting caught might even lead to my arrest for trespassing, I stood at the edge of the Forrester's back yard among a grove of trees for nearly an hour. I only had three days before leaving for the summer, so it was worth the wait.

Lights in each room, even after ten o'clock, remained on in the kitchen and den. When I saw windows brighten upstairs from what I figured was his mother's bedroom, I approached cautiously, set the footstool beneath the den window, and hoisted myself up.

My calculations proved a bit off. Even while arching up, my nose barely cleared the ledge. I looked around behind me, desperate for a log or piece of lawn furniture; nothing.

I lightly tapped a pane. I heard a chuckle, no doubt Everett's bemused surprise at seeing the ski-capped top of my head. I couldn't see in.

"Open it," he whispered loudly.

Slowly, to avoid the wooden creak, I pressed a few fingers under the ridge of a frame.

"Hey," I whispered.

"You nut! Wait a minute."

A crumpled piece of paper hit the window. I heard him mutter, "Damn." On his third attempt, a crudely folded paper plane sailed through the open slit of the window and past me, falling to the ground.

"I leave on Sunday," I whispered. "When can I see you?"

Everett whispered back a command. "Tomorrow. Three o'clock."

I raised my arm, signaled an 'Okay,' before nearly falling backward. I stepped down, grabbed the footstool and the paper plane and snuck off back into the woods.

It wasn't until I had walked home and replaced the footstool in the garage that I pulled the paper from my pocket. Everett had drawn a big outline of a heart. Inside it were cartoon faces of the two of us, our lips elongated in a comic smooch.

Helen snuck me in through the kitchen door as if she were hiding a refugee.

"Eleven years I've worked here. Word gets to the Missus, and I'm on the street."

"Yes, Ma'am."

"Not a word to anyone."

"Yes, Ma'am."

"And no funny business."

"No, Ma'am."

Even though I knew the coast was clear, that we'd face no interruptions or maternal diatribes, I felt cautious as I entered the office-bedroom.

"Jerr-affe."

My expected reply halted when I saw it in a corner; the wheelchair. There wasn't anything unusual about it. The standard metal parts and black seat shone with a new quality. I knew its presence meant hope, in a way. But it also meant more.

"Hey, Monkey," I said, not looking at him.

He saw my stare. "Welcome to my future."

"Wow. Have you tried it?" I approached it, gave it a hesitant touch.

"A little. I'm not ready yet. But, well, that's it."

I pushed aside my awkward reaction and drew close to him. He lay above the sheets in a baggy T-shirt and sweatpants. We hugged carefully, and kissed and touched, until I pulled back as my hand brushed against a small tube that led somewhere between his legs.

"Careful," I said. "Don't want to get your blood pressure up."

"I might burst." His grin seemed to pain him. "Hey, nice haircut."

"Thanks. It's for my job. Didn't want to go in looking like a hippie."

"It's sexy."

"Thanks."

I stood, just taking him in. Unshaven, his hair a bit unkempt, his skin splotchy in a few places, he appeared to be fighting lethargy for my benefit.

"So, I guess you're off to the woods and I'm off to Cripsburgh."

"When are you going?"

"A few weeks. Sit!" He patted his bed. I hesitated. "Don't worry. You can keep your pants on."

"Okay."

"This time."

I settled beside Everett and felt tingles as he affectionately rubbed my crew cut. Even though a few of the smells around him were less than pleasant, as I drew closer, I was relieved to detect his own aroma. I didn't ask him about any medical details. I wanted what might be our last visit together for three months to be good, happy, normal.

"Mom was totally against it at first," he said, absent-mindedly taking my hand, rubbing his stomach with it until I started caressing him. "Until Dad figured out how to make the insurance settlement pay for it, or he's paying part of it. I dunno."

"I hope he's selling a lot of condos."

"Really. So, Dad says this was all your plan."

"Sort of. Kevin kind of inspired it."

"Kev? No way. That dude only thinks with his big dick."

"Actually, he can be a very sensitive, thoughtful guy … with a big dick."

We laughed. I considered going into further detail, but figured he knew. It was practically his idea anyway.

"But you did the footwork," Everett said.

"I guess."

"You really want me to go to this place?"

I cautiously reached my hand up, caressed his face. "I don't want you to go anywhere, but you have to grow, Ev. I'll come visit you."

"Sure you will."

"I will. I could ditch the park job, stay with you. You know I would."

"No. I'll still be here, or there. Where the hell is this place?" He reached for the pile of brochures his father had brought. "Dad picked the one in Piss-bar."

"Well, it's good for us, too. We can all visit you, even your mother."

"Unless you spike her car tires."

"Stop it." I wanted to remind him that despite her dislike toward me, and whatever long-term resentment between them, I did have to thank her for giving birth to this amazing little guy whom I couldn't stop thinking about.

"Hey, do me a favor," he said, adjusting himself in the bed.

"Anything."

"The tree you gave me." He nodded toward the table where it still remained by the window. "Take it somewhere and plant it."

"You don't like it?" I asked in half-mocking disappointment.

"No, no, I love it. You know that. It just … it needs to grow, too."

"Well, where should I put it?"

"You're the nature boy. You'll think of someplace."

"Okay." I retrieved the forlorn little plant, surprised that it hadn't wilted to sticks. Helen had no doubt kept it thriving. Standing before him with it in my hands, I felt a pang of regret, as if he were dismissing me.

"You don't have to do it now. Come here. Helen'll warn us."

"Oh." I put the tree back, and cautiously settled in beside him on the bed.

"Careful of the catheter."

We touched, kissed and caressed each other, but remained clothed. My hands never went lower, partially in deference to Helen's warning. But I also held back, denying my curiosity about his immobile legs.

"So. You're gonna go play mountain man and I'll …"

"Get better."

"Or lung cancer."

"And write me."

"With coal chunks."

"Come on. Will you?"

"Maybe. I get headaches, tired sometimes."

"Don't worry. I just want you to get better."

"No promises. Gotta work the wheelchair."

"That's kind of the goal."

"You know, but the meds," he said softly. "They make my dreams so strange. In one of them, we were together. And we were just walking in the snow, Reid. We were just … walking."

We lay together, misty-eyed, fingers interlocking, wanting to touch so much more, but settling into a half-sleep, as if we were storing up each other's warmth while learning again how to be apart. Two hours later, I left the love of my life, all 18.2 years of it.

EVERY TIME I THINK OF YOU

Chapter 29
Summer, 1979

Everett Forrester
University of Pittsburgh Medical Center
Institute for Rehabilitation & Research
1400 Locust Street Bldg. B, Room 204
Pittsburgh, PA 15219

June 14
Hi, Monkey.

I've finally found some time to write you. I hope you're doing well.

Settling in at the park has been good. I live in a dorm-type cabin with five other people. Our crew includes:

Elliot, our senior ranger. He's nice, about 40, a hunky older dude with a sexy beard (Don't be jealous; ha!). He's basically my boss, but cool about it. He's been working here for almost a decade. He can be a bit obsessive about things, like picking up trash from inconsiderate tourists. But basically, he's cool.

Amanda, who's sort of the assistant senior ranger. She's been working here for a few years and really knows her flora and fauna. I mentioned our recent visit to the Natural History Museum (minus our little, uh, private inter-lewd) and we got into a really fascinating discussion about glacial shifts and geological changes to the region. Well, it was fascinating to us. I'm basically in nerd heaven.

Scott, a graduate student at Pitt, who's focusing on Environmental Studies. He's really charged about fighting nuclear power, went to a few protests back in March after Three Mile Island, and even got arrested! Yeah, he's also a bit of a hunk. Too bad he's not my roommate (See above about the jealousy thing. Besides, I think he's got the hots for Amanda).

Jill, who's too damn perky for her own good, and pretty much inserts being a Christian into every conversation. I've had to watch my words around her, not that I swear or anything, but you know. At least she's the one who gets the church group hikes, which is a relief for me.

Alex, a Vietnamese Botany geek. He's all about hybrids and conservation and studying non-native invasive species. Since he also collects insect samples, hc makes me comparatively non-nerdy. He moved to Philly with about a dozen of his family members when he was five. He's tried to teach me a few words in Vietnamese, but they get caught in my mouth and I don't have a very good memory for languages, I guess. He snores like a buzz saw. I share a room with him.

So, we share a kitchen and a bathroom, all of us. It's kind of cramped, but there's an extra shower outside. I pretty much use that every morning. No, it's enclosed, you perv.

There arc other co-workers who run the gift shop and rangers who spend more time out around the northern regions of the park, but I've only met them briefly, and they either drive home nearby or live at other stations further away where I hope to go camping soon. But for now, I'm kept busy studying maps and learning about giving tours and leading short hikes for the day-trippers.

As you noticed, I'm typing this (duh). Yay! There's an old manual typewriter at the cabin, and a lot of books on nature, so I do some reading and when I want to write you, I can take it outside near the cabin so I don't bother the others at night. Sorry for any typos. I tend to write after sunset with only a Coleman lamp.

It's so beautiful here, Ev. I wish you could visit me. I miss you so much.

I have to tell you I brought a few things like a few small copies of photos Holly took of us, your school sweatshirt (it gets cold at night), and a few other, um, items you sent (grin).

I'll send you some photos when I have time to get them developed. I don't yet have driving privs with the Range Rover, but I go into town a few times with Elliot or Amanda for shopping trips. We have to pay for our own groceries, but Elliot loves cooking, so we go in together for dinners.

For now, enclosed (and probably wilted and flattened, but hey) is a sample of the beautiful wild flowers that abide in the park; Bluets (Houstonia caerulea). I know no one is supposed to pick flowers in a park, but since I work here, I'm giving myself employee privileges. It's amazing to come across a cluster of them, almost like a bed of snow.

Anyway, take care, and write if you can. My phone number's below, but it's in the hallway in our cabin, and not at all private, and there's no answering machine. If you call, which would be best to do in the evening, you can whisper all the sweet nothings you want, but I probably won't be able to whisper much back.

XO, Giraffe

June 23

Yo, Monk!

Still no driving privileges, but I'm keeping busy. I've been relegated to the gate for several days. It's boring, except I get to meet pretty much everyone entering the park on the south side. People mostly know they have to register and pay for camping. I'm basically a cashier and I hand out maps.

Elliot gave me this tip, since he's kind of justifiably paranoid about smokers. When he works the gate, he looks in the car for an open ashtray or a trace of cigarettes, then gives a stronger version of the fire safety lecture. Most people are cool.

Others, like the fathers —who are almost always the driver, so I talk to them— think they know everything, even though I'm required to recite my safety scripts.

No, there are no bears, Booboo. But there are a lot of scavenging animals that like to pig out on people food. Makes a mess if campers don't lock up their food. I had to play janitor at three campsites. It upsets me how sometimes people can be so careless.

There's a busload of kids from Erie coming up, I mean down, for the day next week. Elliot said I could give a talk on park safety and how not to get lost, all the plants and animals to see, that sort of thing. I'm kind of nervous about talking in front of our first group of kids. Wish me luck!

Your flower of the week is Woodpoppy (Stylophorum diphyllum). Its leaves are kind of rough, like kale, but the blossoms are (or were; by the time you get them they'll be brown) a bright deep yellow.

XO, Reid

June 28

Everino,

Well, the kids' talk went really well. I was nervous at first, wondering if I'd run out of things to say, but they have so many questions! I mean, it's amazing. They're so curious! Of course, I got totally upstaged when Rick, this guy with the fire prevention crew, came by in a Smokey the Bear costume. He does these appearances for the kids' groups, and can't really talk under his bear suit. So I kind of interpret for him. It's hilarious. The kids all want to hug him and we take their pictures with him. It's just so great knowing we're teaching these little kids to love nature and respect da erf, ya know?

Actually, knowing there's a cute guy underneath the bear outfit makes it kinda hot.

Yes, I am a total perv.

Yours in arboreal affection,

Ranger Reid

PS: your wildflower this time is Turtlehead, aka Chelone glabra, not to be confused with Lyon's Turtlehead, aka Chelone lyoni. Wouldn't want there to be any confusion. Besides, the Lyon's Turtlehead have thick blossoms, and I'll need a box to mail you one of those.

July 1

Everett Evergreen,

Hey, my sexy man, How are you? Ain't heard from you, so I hope you're okay and enjoying my silly letters. You know you can call me at night, too.

Enclosed are a few photos of me. I hope you appreciate the pics of me shirtless in my hot ranger shorts and hat and boots. I basically had to come out to Elliot, since I didn't want my roommate Alex knowing just yet that I'm a homo. I figured Elliot would be cool about it, and he was. He asked if the pics were for a girl back home, and I told him no. He didn't push it, but I just blurted out, "They're for my boyfriend." He laughed and took a few extras, so I guess he's cool.

But, you know, I hope you don't mind me calling you my boyfriend. I'm not sure what we are, except you're the most important person to me. Well, you know, I'm supposed to think that about my parents, and in reality, the people you're with are important, which makes my co-workers important. But anyway, I hope you know how I feel about you and that I miss you.

Speakin' of which, we had a totally amazing rainstorm the other day. Practically, it was good, because believe it or not, people have been known to camp over July 4 holiday and set off fireworks – I know, idiotic, right? – and the woods are damp and wet and safer. The major cause of wildfires is lightning,

Elliot said, and he was more worried about that, so there were a lot of phone calls with the ranger station further north, but fortunately no fires.

But the amazing thing was my little private adventure. I was out by myself when the afternoon rain hit. Some late campers had arrived before the gates closed for the night, and I'd warned them of the impending storm.

On my walk back to our cabin, the first droplets began to fall, light at first, then in heavy splats. Instead of hightailing it to shelter, I veered into the woods and off the trail. I've become pretty adept at going off-trail. My sense of direction's become pretty good. And you know, it may sound odd, but I think looking at all these wide scenic views has improved my eyesight. I've been ditching the glasses more often.

I found this mossy grove near a stream, and the trees provided enough shelter, with just a light sprinkling of the rain coming down. The darkened skies gave the grove a beautiful glow.

Knowing I was completely alone, it didn't take much for the longing to rise. I peeled off my ranger duds, and in just my boots and socks (Is this sounding familiar?) I had the most intense experience. It wasn't just whacking off, you know? It was like I was communing with the trees, the moss and lichen, the wild flowers, the sod made of the remnants of wild animals from a hundred thousand years ago. Once I started thinking of you, and how great it would be to have you there, it got more intense.

Ev, I have these feelings for you that just won't go away. I know we have to be apart, and I don't know what's gonna happen, but just know, every time I think of you...

Your wild flower this time is the Common Blue Violet (Viola papilonacea). Believe me, Monkey, when I found them, it wasn't common at all.

Your Giraffe

July 12
Ev, Ever, Every, Everett.
Wow.
Wow, wow, wow.
Thank you SOO MUCH for the tape!! It's so great to hear your voice. You're a real great storyteller. That part where you gave me an audio tour of the facility was funny, especially when you dropped the tape recorder.

I understand about you not being able to write much. It sounds like they're keeping you busy with the physical therapy. I didn't realize there would be older people at the rehab center, but it makes sense. Really, your accompanist is 73? She sure can tickle the ivories. It sounds like you were all having a really good time. Do you do that very often?

It was very considerate of your mom to bring sheet music. I didn't know you could sing so well! Well, I did, but not with so many Cole Porter songs. Pretty amazing. You are so talented. Did you ever do that at home at that big piano I saw?

It's nice to hear that Holly's been visiting you, too. She was so nice to me. It means a lot. You know she was the only person who called me after your accident. I really think of her as a sister. I hope to see her again soon when I visit, not until late August, of course. But the first thing I'll do is hop on the train to Piss-bar and see you.

I've been listening to your tapes so much (I still have the other one), I had to give Amanda some extra money for more batteries on her last shopping trip. Sometimes I listen to it in bed with my earphones while Alex is snoring. Okay, that last part where you sing and talk so softly? I admit it, I did rub one out a few times. Just hearing your voice makes me all mushy inside. Well, not mushy in a certain anatomical area.

Your flower this time is Rue Anemone (Anemonella thalictroides). Cute, aren't they? So tiny, yet so pretty.

XXO, Reidster

July 19

Ev, Everything,

I finally saw the most amazing deer. I know, it's about time, right? In fall, they're littering up the side of the highways like roadkill. Well, not like roadkill, but actual roadkill. But in summer, they're pretty discreet. I've seen a few others animals, mostly birds: geese, osprey, owls, swallows and a few others. There was talk of a bear sighting, so I was wrong about that. Of course, we've seen raccoons, but mostly just around the garbage dumpsters. They're locked to keep them out, but the smell of food draws them.

But the deer. Wow.

See, I had finally set up my tent in a remote part of the park the tourists aren't supposed to use. It's blocked off because the road leading to it isn't safe for cars since the rainstorm. But I knew the trail to get there, and got permission from Elliot to set up my tent and a few supplies. I've been spending a few nights a week out there. I had a dose of cabin fever, since, well, I'm living in a cabin.

Basically, it's all your fault. No, I'm joking, sort of.

It was on a Saturday night, and we had this big dinner. Elliot made barbequed chicken breasts, and Amanda made this enormous salad. We had a little wine, except Jill, because she's a Christian, which made no sense to me, since Jesus was the one who made wine so popular. But anyway, Jill, who's a Christian, reminds us of it at least once a day. Thank her god she likes being all perky with the tourists, and is usually elsewhere in the visitor center or thankfully acres away from me.

The rest of us got a little buzzed, especially Alex, who didn't have much drinking experience. We got to talking about improvements and construction that are planned for the park (long after I'll be gone). The first thing that popped out of my mouth was making the trails more accessible for the handicapped. And Jill went off on this bizarre tangent about God's will and even though Jesus loves the crippled (Don't you feel lucky?), she started babbling about "dominion over the lands," how only people who were hardy enough to hike deserved to enjoy the upper and outlying parts of the park, so I just went off on her.

I called you my best friend, but gave a little glance at Elliot. He knew that you were the reason I got him to take those shirtless photos of me. So we're more than friends. Right?

Jill's point of view was shot down by Elliot and Amanda, who tried to play mediator. But I got a bit angry and said how wrong it was that you couldn't enjoy this beautiful park in all its glory without some kind of mule pack dragging you along.

I'm sorry if that's offensive or anything. I was kind of drunk.

Alex had no opinion, was practically asleep already from the wine, and he's more interested in bugs.

That's why I'm typing this from my little campsite with nobody around. And this morning, I emerged from my tent, stark naked with a pee boner, and there, about twenty feet away from me, was this beautiful, perfect immense stag, with about seven points on his antlers. We locked eyes for about a minute. I froze, wishing I had my camera, until he darted away and disappeared.

So, thank you for indirectly causing all this.

Ranger Reid, naked in the woods

PS: I finally got some larger envelopes, so here's a big one; Pickerel Weed (Pontederia cordata). Pretty neat, huh?

August 12

Ev.

Sorry it's been so long since I've written. Thank you for the postcard.

It's hot. And humid.

Oh, and I caught Scott naked in the outdoor shower. That's pretty much the only interesting thing that's happened. Yeah, he's banging Amanda. From what I saw in the shower, she's got good taste.

Jill has left our fair company a bit sooner than expected, probably to join a nunnery.

But enough stupid gossip. Let me tell you about the moon.

Since roommate Alex's snoring continues (actually, he does settle down to a mild buzz, eventually), and my earphones always fall off in bed, I've taken to sneaking out of the cabin for some night hikes. It's so amazing.

Yes, I do strip down to just my boots. Yes, I am a nature perv. Yes, I think about you and wish you could be with me when I hike up to the peak of nearby mountaintops, slightly winded, my sweat glistening in the moonlight. But you can't be jealous of the moon, can you?

Seeing the vista, the green rolling hills, and once even, taking a cautious nighttime dip in a stream, it's like I get completely lost, disembodied and yet so in touch with my body. I can't explain it, but I'm trying. Naming a faith, a belief, is so beside the point when I hear some nearby animal rustling in the bushes, and get startled, then comforted, being so alone, yet completely filled with the presence of the glow of moonlight on the plants and the water. A few times I've gone rutting like some lone stag, or just lain in a bank or rubbed myself on a mossy tree stump, which I don't recommended, unless you like ants on your butt.

The point is, I found god or whatever, you know, like you said that night in the woods at Pinecrest.

But then, I'll hike back downhill, waiting to get dressed until I'm close to a campsite or the cabins, and take a peek at the photo Holly took (she made a wallet-sized and a big one; that's back at home), and I see you and me together, you kissing the top of my head, and I curse that same god that made your accident happen.

I know you said you've forgiven what's his name who hit you on the field. But it's such a struggle, trying to make peace with it. So much beauty and so much misfortune.

Yes, I think I'm going a little crazy. I feel like my whole body and mind have changed.

Your flora of the week, quite the red beauty, is the Cardinal Flower (Lobelia cardinalis).

See you in a few weeks.

Love, Reid

Chapter 30

Returning home took some adjustment. All the buildings and roads, cars and gas stations struck me as extraordinarily ugly, almost obscene.

My parents welcomed me with enthusiasm, of course, and obligatory hugs. They marveled over my tan and my "rugged" new look, as Mom called it. I had barely seen myself all summer, other than perfunctory bathroom mirror glances.

Once fed, chatted out, and alone in my room, I took a long look at myself, naked, standing in front of the long mirror attached to my inside clothes closet door, and agreed. My hair had lightened and the trace of my day-old stubble was more pronounced. It was as if I'd grown a few inches, or browned to ripeness. I looked almost like a man.

Forced to wait a few days before my visit to Everett in Pittsburgh, I had to fill out university forms and select a course schedule. Once again, I called Holly in advance, asked to stay over. She said she'd give me a copy of her house keys.

I thanked Dad for the offer of a ride to the train station, but instead made a light job of it with my backpack over my shoulders. In the late August heat, I wore shorts and a T-shirt. I read a book on the train, eagerly anticipating my visit. Outside the window, along the train tracks, oak and elm trees stood tall in between the majority of evergreens.

When I arrived at Holly's apartment, she warned me that Everett had been in a bad mood the past few weeks.

"He's been really resistant to the physical therapy sessions. They tried a few different med combinations," she said as we ate a makeshift lunch of sandwiches. "But the anti-depressants made him constipated. The steroids make him moody, and then they said they might operate again, and it got all our hopes up, but then they changed their minds, and, well. He's not a happy camper."

"Well, I guess it's been rough for him."

"It's not just that. He–" Holly hesitated, fidgeted with her sandwich, then dropped it. "He's had episodes before."

"Episodes?"

"He gets depressed and angry, like when our dad left, and a few other times. It's not like he's crazy or anything."

"Well, a little of the good crazy."

"Well, yeah, but... He doesn't react well when things don't go the way he wants them to. He's kind of been in denial about not recovering, and it's all kind of finally sunk in."

While I took in her concerns, inside I was still determined. I was going to see my guy, and was full of hope. I would cheer him up.

But as I took the pair of buses to get downtown, I saw Pittsburgh through Everett's eyes, as one steep hill after another. How would he get around without depending on others? Who wouldn't be angry?

The rehabilitation center was smaller than I'd expected, a two-story building adjoining the larger hospital. After signing in at the front desk, I followed the directions, passed patients of different ages scooting by in wheelchairs, and even saw a recreation room where I guessed his little music concert had taken place.

After following the succession of room numbers, I found his door open, and gave it a light knock.

"Hey," he said casually as he turned in his wheelchair. I stepped toward him and leaned down to hug him.

"I missed you so much. How are you?"

"Oh," he shrugged. "You know."

I looked around, eager to find some excuse for an upbeat comment. A cross between a dorm room and a private hospital suite, Everett –or someone else– had added a few personal touches to what had become his temporary home. Framed pictures showed a few Parisian scenes and drawings, assuring me that Holly had become the default makeshift decorator. Above his bed, the Styx *Grand Illusion* poster with those enchanted woods had been put up with tacks.

"Almost homey," I half-joked.

"Yeah, Holly did some of that," he said in a tired tone of voice. "Mom and Helen brought a bunch of stuff. It's like they just want someplace prettier to visit."

All the fixtures, light switches and handles were lower, while power outlets were raised, making for a slightly disorienting feeling. I felt both taller and shorter than normal.

While a small counter top and mid-level cabinet shelf were crammed with boxes of cereal and other food, there wasn't a stove, just a small low sink with room underneath for a wheelchair. The linoleum floor retained a hospital feel. But there was no trace of the medicinal air. It smelled of him, perhaps due to the overstuffed laundry bag in a corner.

"I brought some stuff." I extracted a pile of pamphlets and brochures, all from Temple University. "Did you know the mascot's an owl? Pretty funny, huh?"

Rambling on about the scholarship potential for disabled students, seeing other wheelchair students and the layout of the campus, I hadn't noticed that since I'd been in the room, Everett had remained unmoving, his face knotted into a scowl.

"I don't know if I even want to go to college."

"Why not? Holly told me you graduated."

"They mailed me some tests and then I got a diploma. Big deal. What's the use?"

"The use? The use is you're smart and you've got your whole life ahead of you."

"You sound like my damn counselor, Miss Happy Thoughts."

"I'm sorry."

"Why are you sorry? You didn't do this."

"I know." I wiped my eyes, surprised by the sudden tears.

"Oh, don't cry again, please? The guy, from the other team who hit me, Chris, came to visit me, and just could not stop bawling. His parents dragged him here, told me they were praying for me. What the hell is that gonna do? It's like I'm responsible for everybody else being fucked up."

This was turning out to be a really unpleasant visit. I hovered over him, hoping to offer another sympathetic hug or perhaps a kiss. He gently pushed me off.

"Look, I appreciate all your help and everything, but if I do go to school, it's probably going to be at Carnegie Mellon."

"What?"

"My dad asked me to move in with him here in Pittsburgh after I get released, and, well, the house in Greensburg isn't right. I hate using his old office as my bedroom, and Mom won't ... It just makes sense."

"Oh." Although he'd never said he would definitely go to school, or even with me, I was stunned by my presumption that he would want to be close to me. Trying to make light of this news, I said, "Well, I'll visit you on holidays, I guess, and make more visits home. It's not that long a trip."

Actually, it was seven hours, provided the trains from Philadelphia were running on time. For a moment, I thought to consider abruptly changing my plans, perhaps going to the University of Pittsburgh instead. They hadn't offered me a scholarship, but I couldn't bear being apart from him again.

"Yeah, see, Reid, the thing is ..."

Anticipating what he was going to say, my reaction strangely began in my nose, like a sniffle, then moved to my throat, a clenching feeling that plummeted down to my stomach.

"I think maybe we need some time apart."

"I just spent all summer away from you. What are you–"

"Maybe I should just let you go."

"Go where? If you want me to leave, I'll come back later."

"No, I don't mean just now. Those letters, your mountain adventures. I know you were trying to cheer me up, but it just made me realize … That's your future, your dream. I can't be a part of that, like this."

"That's not my whole life, Ev. Besides, there are plenty of campsites we could drive to. I mean, maybe we can't hike, exactly, but I can haul you on my back. I'll get sled dogs!"

He sighed, as if even faking a smile were too exhausting. "You need to go live your life."

My mind reeled. If it hadn't been for me, he'd still be lying on a bed in that makeshift bedroom in Forrestville; Miss Havisham, but a guy. "Oh. You mean go *away* away."

"You know, Reid, I'm never gonna be what I was."

"I never said you should. But I want to be with you. I missed you so much. Please–"

"Why are you so needy? I should be the one whining."

"Like you're not already?"

"You need to … let go."

"But you're the only guy I've ever–"

"That. Is. The point."

I struggled to understand, blurting out the first thing that came to me. "Well, I guess I can't see the Forrester for the trees."

Visibly annoyed, he muttered, "That's my dad's joke, and it's not funny."

I stood, waiting, frightened of him, for him.

"Everything's changed," he almost shouted.

"I know that."

"I don't think you do."

"Look, what is this? You sounded so upbeat in the tape you made for me."

"That was when I still had some hope."

"For what?"

"What do you think?" he shouted, incredulous at my ignorance as he pounded his thighs with his fists before forcing himself to calm down. "I want to ask you, Reid." His eyes twisted to narrow slits, almost accusative. I'd never seen him so angry. "Some people are saying I won't heal. Ever. Others hope so. What do you think?"

"I–"

"Because if you're one of those who hopes I'll change back, who will never look at me the same way again if I won't, then I don't think we can be together."

"Ev, please."

"Look, I can't ... We can't even do it, like maybe ever."

"You think this is just about sex? This is about friendship, too."

"Reid. You need to ... think about a life that isn't just about me."

"I can't believe this." The tears sprang out. "You..." I gestured toward him with a movement I would regret for months. "... are breaking up with me."

"What was that?"

"What?"

"That!" Everett repeated my gesture with an angry jab. "Like I'm supposed to be grateful? Like you're the one who does the dumping, because you're not in a chair?"

"No, I'm sorry. No, I didn't mean–"

"Yes, you did."

"No, I didn't."

"Then, what did you mean?"

Lips pressed together, I stared at the ceiling. Okay, if it was over, he was going to get the full dose.

"What I meant," I slowed down, found a place to sit, to be at his level, so that he wouldn't feel overwhelmed, loomed over. "What I meant was how upsetting it is that you take this all so casually, the fact that I'm just totally ... love you."

Everett said something in Latin.

I didn't ask him to translate.

"From the first day I met you," I said, attempting to stay calm, "I thought, here is this guy who's wild enough to be right there, where I would be wild. I thought, wow, I got so lucky, right off the bat; first time and he's ... But that same day, the way you turned so casual. There wasn't a minute that I thought of you and wondered, when will this end? When will he realize what a dork I am? I guess that's ... now."

Everett sat, his arms folded tight, waiting. He could have left. I knew to let that happen, that wheeling away is the right of a person.

"You should go back to Kevin."

"Kevin?" I almost shouted. I stood, turning away to see a woman with a clipboard held against her chest standing at the open door, giving me a stern glare.

"Is everything okay in there?" she asked.

"Yes, we're fine," Everett hissed. "Could you close the door, please?"

She did.

I lowered my voice to a simmer. "You practically threw him at me, as what? Some kind of substitute? He's just a ... He's a nice guy, sure, but Jeez, Ev."

"You need to–"

I drew closer to him. "You know what I need? If you have any other boyfriends who take trains and bang up cars and break into houses and get drunk and practically fuck in front of your parents, one at a time, if you recall, just to be with you, I'd really like to meet him. He sounds like a great guy."

Everett slumped in his chair even lower. Regretting my scolding tone, I tried to inject a little humor. "I mean, come on. You mailed me your jock strap. If that's not love, what is?"

At least that got a smile out of him.

"I'm trying to understand what you're going through. Just ... just help me."

"Do you wanna try it?" Everett wheeled backward to a chair, as if to remove himself from his own. "Go out for a spin. See how far you get before your shoulders cramp and your fingers get caught in the spokes and your piss bag spills and some old lady three times your age asks if you 'need some help, sweetie?'"

Crouching down before him, I put my hands on his knees, despite realizing he couldn't feel me there. I said, softly, "You helped me."

"What?"

"Ev, since I met you ..." I couldn't explain how he'd inspired me, driven me to grow, and by loving him love myself. "I know everything's changed, but I want to be here for you. It's what I want."

Intent on staring at some point on the floor, he muttered, "This is not about you."

"Oh, okay."

"No, Reid. It's not okay. It's about what I'm going through. It's about losing everything physical I just took for granted, and it's falling off my chair when I'm just trying to put my socks on. It's not fun, and it's not sexy and it's just ... not."

And then Everett said what I hoped was a lie. Not one of the many small charming fibs that got him what he wanted, or into trouble, which he also liked. It was what I hoped was his one great lie.

"I don't love you like you want me to."

Trying to figure out which parts of him could still feel, and which parts had voluntarily shut down, I offered a hesitant, cautious hug.

"Well, I love you like I want to."

"Just go home. We'll talk later."

We didn't, for three months.

Chapter 31
Autumn, 1979

My freshman semester at Temple University was spent trying to focus on my studies, to make new friends, and to not think about Everett. In that last effort, I failed miserably.

Not that there weren't ample distractions in a two-bedroom, four-guy dorm with a common area that almost every weekend erupted into drinking and semi-naked hijinks that never resulted in, to use a sports term, follow-through.

I had been fortunate enough to have Eric, one of my three dorm mates, turn out to be easy-going and a lot like me. A husky ex-jock who actually liked studying, between his biology major and my own, we found an equal fascination somewhere between cells and seeds.

Initially separated, we had decided to change our initial room assignments after a few days. Our collective poster decoration clearly showed that our similarities and differences made the decision a good one.

Eric's décor was mostly *Star Wars* and other science fiction movie posters, while my wall became adorned with a map from Allegheny State Park and a poster of the Amazon rain forest I'd bought at the student bookstore. Charlie and Dennis, in the adjoining suite, favored posters of Cheryl Tiegs and Farrah Fawcett, among a few more revealing female centerfolds.

For me, the dormitory's showers proved to be an infrequent boner-friendly environment. A few guys on my dorm floor had occasionally displayed themselves behind not-completely closed shower curtains.

Eric's invitations to join him in workouts at the school gym provided more fascinating distractions. The main locker room's environment turned out to be cautiously flirtatious, while Eric, who was straight, seemed oblivious or dismissive. I limited my timid cruising to lone visits.

I did become distracted by the frequent possibility of furtive sex with strangers, but never took it to completion. I never stopped thinking of Everett. I just put him aside, until I would see or hear a reminder.

One night my roommates decided to drag me off to one of the local bars on a Saturday night, claiming I was studying too hard. Somewhere after the second shared pitcher of beer, one of those anthem-like songs by Styx blasted through the speakers. The guys started singing along, hoisting their mugs.

"I'm okay! I finally found the person I've been searching for!"

The tears just sprang out of my eyes, right in front of the guys. Even though I didn't tell them why I was so upset, they seemed sympathetic, but I just left.

Wobbling my way back to the dorm, I thought of that Styx poster in Everett's bedroom and at the rehab center, and how I never even thought to ask him if he'd seen them perform, or if he'd gone to concerts with Kevin as I had done a few times. What if we both had, and I'd met him then, and later on somehow managed to get him to ditch that one lacrosse game for another of our secretive meetings?

There were other less convoluted reminders. Several students in wheelchairs lived on campus. The sight of each one of them brought a pang of longing to me. I withheld the frequent desire to walk up to them, burst out with pride some kind of pronouncement that would endear me to them. *Hey, the guy I love is in a wheelchair! Let's be friends!*

Instead, I simply made eye contact and greeted those that returned my look with a simple 'Hi.' Most times, after their initial surprise, they returned a greeting after the second or third time.

While sitting at the cafeteria, eating a sandwich while highlighting text in my Botany 101 book, I noticed one of those students, a young Black guy in a wheelchair, had rolled up beside me.

"This seat taken?"

"Oh. No."

He seemed to appreciate my gesture of pulling the chair next to me away to another table to make room for him. He rolled closer, placed a paper bag on the table next to me. His pants were baggy around his legs. I made a quick estimate as to the level of his injury's location.

"Devon." He pronounced it 'di-VON.' We shook hands. I felt a pang of guilt for sizing him up for what I thought was wrong with him before actually seeing him.

"Reid."

"Botany?"

"Yep."

"You like plants."

"We get along," I grinned.

"You a freshman?"

"Yep. You?"

"Sophomore." He said it like 'south-more.'

We made small talk about classes and the campus before Devon segued to his real reason for introducing himself.

"So, a couple of my friends, you know, other wheelchair peeps, noticed you."

"Oh? How so?"

"Well, you been a little more friendly than most of the students. To us. Almost like on purpose. You in campus politics or something?"

I smiled, shaking my head, while measuring my resolve, and how much I thought it wise to share.

"No, I, uh, have a friend who's, uh, handicapped."

"He go here?"

"No. He's at a rehab facility in Pittsburgh." I swallowed, breathed. "Actually, he's my boyfriend, sort of. We're kind of not–"

"Oh, oh, that's cool. You got a thing for crips?"

"What? Oh, no. No, we, we dated before. It's not–"

"Cool. What happened to him?"

I explained Everett's lacrosse accident, surprising myself with my compacted and outwardly emotionless account of the events.

Devon had been in a car crash in North Philadelphia late one night. He went into a lot of details about it, and his struggle to recover. He didn't have the advantage of a wealthy family, or much of a family, and the guy driving the car had a few violations, plus lapsed car insurance, yet survived the accident with merely a few sprains. Devon was basically left with state and local services, which in themselves had been a hassle to get.

"Then my case worker found out about the scholarships here, and it's been a lot smoother," Devon finished his story. "Sorry, I'm talkin' too much."

"No, no, it's cool." I closed my book.

We ate our food, talked of other things that had nothing to do with wheelchairs or accidents. Devon offered to show me around the off-campus bars he liked, which meant those that didn't have stairs. We traded numbers and left the cafeteria together. Before heading off in opposite directions, Devon said, "Good luck with your friend."

"Thanks."

"I hope you get to see him soon."

"I hope so, too."

"He'd be lucky to have you."

Before meeting Devon, I was about to the point where I could last an entire day without thinking about Everett. At night, in my mind, I was all his.

Running had come back to me. Starting off with a few loops around the outdoor track at school, I politely declined invitations to join an intramural group of guys. Running off-campus around city blocks was just too difficult, so I branched off to a few trails that looped the campus. The autumnal clusters of trees reminded me of my summer in the state park, and I relaxed.

The good pain in my legs and lungs returned. My pacing felt steady, my mind at ease to later dive into my studies. For several weeks, I had deceived myself into thinking I could move on with my life.

Pulling my textbooks for the day from my backpack, I stacked them on my desk for another night of studying, before a hoped-for nap and before my other two noisier dorm-mates returned.

My roommate Eric and I shared a small corkboard on the wall between our desks. I saw a small piece of scrap paper tacked to the board with a familiar phone number and name: 'Holly.'

Weighing the burden of returning her call, I fought the surge of conflicted feelings that rose. Was it more bad news about Everett? Good news? Had he miraculously healed? Had he tried to kill himself? I'd read in my research phase months before that the suicide rate among some disabled people was far higher than among the able-bodied.

Did Holly want my mailing address to send more heart-wrenching photos of him, pictures that would only remind me of what I'd lost? The ones I had were filed away in a sealed envelope at the bottom of a desk drawer. Several times I had considered just mailing them to myself back home, wishing I'd left them hidden away.

Pacing around my room, unable to either study or nap, my steps turned into a walk out of the dorm, which became a run, a sloppy aimless tear. I wasn't even dressed properly; in jeans, a shirt, a jacket and sneakers that weren't for running. Exhausted, panting, one of my calves spasming with a cramp, I found a quiet glen of trees and lay on the ground amid a carpet of brilliant orange oak leaves.

Once I'd hobbled back to my room, I peeled off my sweaty clothes and donned a towel as I headed off to the communal showers. Letting the hot water almost scald my back, I told myself I was letting the remnants of concern for Everett circle the drain. My skill at telling minor lies, taught by him so expertly, worked best when self-directed.

Almost parboiled from the shower, I returned to my room. Eric would probably be back soon. I would have a little time for privacy.

"I should be really pissed off at you," Holly said as soon as I found the nerve to call. Not a 'Hello,' not a 'How's school?'

"What happened?"

"Nothing happened to him, physically. He's fine."

"Oh, good."

"It's not that, Reid. He refuses to so much as look at the application forms for Carnegie Mellon. Dad's pissed off. Mom is livid."

"Your mother spends a lot of time being livid."

"That's how she stays so skinny," she chuckled.

"The last time I visited, he said he had doubts about college. You think he's just afraid?"

"No, he's not. He just doesn't want to stay here in Pittsburgh, or go back to Greensburg."

"And how is that my fault?"

"Have you talked to him recently?"

"No. He..." He drove me away, I wanted to say. "I thought that was up to him."

"Well, it is, sort of," she agreed. "And I understand. I even offered to move to another apartment, you know, first-floor without stairs, so he could live with me. Mom said she'd already made sure they had an accessible dorm room for him. But she's planning –get this– to move to Pittsburgh if she sells the house."

"I bet your dad's thrilled."

"Well, we all want to be near him and support him."

"That's good," I said.

"It would be, if it would help him, but he'd just … He needs to grow the fuck up."

"And being surrounded by his family isn't–"

"Exactly," she said.

"You want him around, don't you?"

"Of course I do. But he needs … Look, I don't know if I should tell you this."

I wasn't sure what to expect from a woman who considered her abortion to be an appropriate breakfast conversation topic.

"I visited him a few days ago, and he's really getting himself together. But we were gabbing away, it was getting late, and I mentioned you, and he just cracked. He'd been holding himself together, being brave, but he just started sobbing out of nowhere."

"Was it his meds?"

"No, Reid. It was you."

"Me?"

"He's really sorry about the fight you had," she said. "He misses you a lot. A lot. When you guys visited me, it wasn't just some mini-vacation. He was bringing you to meet me for approval, something he could never do with our parents. He's never done that before."

I wondered how many other events we'd shared meant more to him, and why I hadn't seen behind his casual attitude.

"You have to understand," she said. "From here on, people are seeing the wheelchair first. You're not like that. We're not."

At that moment, as the expected rush of emotion and the fought-back tears emerged from months of bottled-up longing, my roommate Eric bounded into our room. I didn't even need to signal him. Seeing the phone in my hand and the contorted look on my face, he just plopped his backpack on the floor and closed the door behind him as he retreated.

"Sorry," I sniffed. "What did you say?"

"If he asked for you, if he wanted to be with you, would you? Would you be there for him?"

Hadn't I already shown that? Hadn't I, with my nearly incompetent romantic skills, done everything I could to love him?

"I… I have to think about that."

"Okay. I'm not going to push it. But can I at least give the little brat your address?"

A few days later, a card arrived in the mail, one of those corny store-bought themed ones with a bashful cartoon character holding a tiny bouquet of flowers.

Folded into the envelope was a flyer for 'The Fourth Annual Thanksgiving Weekend Wheelchair Basketball Tournament.'

Beside the date and address was scribbled:

Please visit. Miss you.
XO, Monkey.
PS: I'm much better! No more rage fits.
And bring a swimsuit.

Chapter 32

Greg tossed the basketball with a flair some NBA players might have envied, considering he had a few feet more to reach. His shaggy brown hair clung to his brow with sweat. The tattoos on one arm, exposed by his sleeveless jersey, and his Doobie Brothers mustache added to his handsome charm. The way he wheeled himself across the court with such flair and abandon drew me to him.

A Vietnam veteran who had started the roving basketball league years before the rehabilitation facility even existed, Greg was clearly the most experienced player on the court. With only four men for each team —actually one of them a woman, Grace, whom I would also meet that day— the competition was more compressed than those I'd watched in high school, and the game was accented by the tire squeaks and metal clash of wheelchairs.

Grace was one of the few players who fell hard during the course of the game. When it happened to Everett, I felt a lurch in my chest.

But each of them struggled, then finally got back up, and the game continued. The few times Everett got the ball, he sped up, fumbled, but improved as the game continued.

The game over (Everett's team lost by a few dozen points, but didn't seem to care), they wheeled themselves over to various friends and family members who sat on the bleachers. Several other outpatients, who had formed a loose line along the front row, wheeled into smaller congratulatory circles.

Everett and I high- or, more precisely, mid-fived, but his arm caught my side and pulled me lower toward him. I attempted a hug, but he held me closer and pushed a sweaty kiss that landed closer to my neck than its intended target. His scraggly attempt of a beard itched, but felt good.

I hadn't realized or even considered the possibility of being openly affectionate with him in front of others there. With sweat clinging to his hair, which had grown out into curly ringlets, his face beamed, despite his team having been thrashed. He grabbed me closer and gave the kiss a do-over.

"So, is this the biped you're dating?" Greg teased as he toweled off near us while sizing me up.

"Yep," Everett grinned.

Considering we hadn't seen each other in months, dating wasn't exactly the best description. While I was hoping for a passionate reunion, I had prepared myself for a disappointing redefinition of our bond as mere friends. But I didn't correct him.

"Well, to each his own," Greg sighed. He caught me looking at his flexing tanned arms as he raised one, then the other, switching hands with the towel as he wiped his pits. "Better keep him on a short leash," Greg said as he tossed his towel at me. I caught it as I chuckled, a bit embarrassed.

"*Quisque comodeus est.*"

Everett was showing off again. I knew my line. "Which translates to...?"

"Everybody's a comedian."

"So, why didn't you invite your family?" I asked.

"Holly's been up before a few times. Took some great pictures. Gotta show ya."

"Sweet."

"She and the parents were up here on Thursday for Thanksgiving; took me out to some fancy restaurant. God, the waiter made such a fuss. What a queen. He probably would have cut up my food if I'd asked. Besides, I wanted to save today for you."

His invitation had put such a surge of anticipation into me that the seven hours spent on a train from Philadelphia to home that week kept me in such a hopeful mood, my parents mistook my joy for a cured bout of homesickness.

I'd waited until after Thanksgiving dinner to tell them of my weekend plans. The series of expressions my mother made at the table had shifted from confusion to dismay to a resigned false indifference. It was clear she wanted to protect me from any pain, but knew I'd go anyway. My dad merely offered his car, saying, "The trains are probably too slow over the holidays."

After I got to Pittsburgh, we'd only had a few minutes to talk and re-establish some kind of connection before Everett had to take to the court for his eventual joyful defeat. He'd met me in the lobby of the facility and I'd followed him across the street to the gym. He had acted more open and energetic, but the situation prevented any closer connection.

"I need a shower," Everett said as he placed his small towel in his backpack, then reached around to hang it on his chair.

This wasn't the depressed, angst-ridden soul who'd dismissed me only a few months before. His body pumped with vitality and color. It was sexy, life-affirming. He was transformed.

"A shower?" I asked. "What do you do, just ride under them in the locker room?"

"Bad joke," he said in mock disdain. "You'll have to do better. Why don't you come up to my room and help me?"

And then I saw that flirtatious glint in his eyes. Before I was able to ask if he meant what I'd hoped, a short young Indian woman approached.

"Oh, this is Daya, my physiotherapist."

"Reid." We shook hands.

"Pleased to meet you." She knelt down to inspect Everett's arms, then his legs. "How are you feeling? Do you think you got any injuries?"

"No, I'm fine. I'm fine."

"Okay." She didn't seem convinced.

"You don't have to go back with me," Everett said.

"You're going to dinner, yes?" she insisted, giving me a look, as if requesting consent.

"Yes, Daya," Everett said. "I'll be alright. Lemme hang with my guy, okay?"

His guy. That was a good sign.

"Remember; exercise tomorrow, and swimming."

"Yes. Thank you, Daya."

"It was nice to meet you," she nodded before leaving us.

"See?" Everett smiled. "You're staying over, right?"

"Uh…"

"We'll take care of you at reception. I get a free room pass a few times a month. You probably have to sleep in a guest room, though."

"I could just take the bus back to Holly's," I said, my expectations on hold.

"Suit yourself."

Following him across the campus and up to his room, it seemed obvious that he had come to terms with his situation, even if I hadn't.

After we'd closed his door, he tossed off his sweaty jersey, at least making that shot into a laundry bag. The weather that day had been warm for November, and late afternoon sunlight gave the room a golden tint.

"This is new," I said, gesturing toward a pull-up bar that had been installed over the bathroom doorway.

"Oh, yeah. Check it out." He turned and backed under the bar, then pulled himself up and down more than a dozen times before plopping himself back down to his chair. His chest muscles, tightened from the exertion, glistened with sweat.

"Damn."

"Yeah, it's good for the guns." He flexed his arms. As my memory flashed back to that first Polaroid he had sent me, he leaned down and removed his shoes and socks with some minor effort.

"You might as well get naked, too," he smiled as he wheeled into the bathroom. The wide door led to an even wider bathroom and toilet with steel bars at each side. "Gimme a few minutes. I gotta empty my pee bag and stuff."

"Doesn't that ... hurt?"

"What?"

"Taking it out?"

"Well, no, since I can't feel my dick," he called out from the bathroom. "Besides, I got a different one, called a Texas catheter. It's like a rubber; doesn't go inside. Wanna see?"

"Not just yet!"

"Okay!"

Relieved that Everett had achieved a degree of patience with my ignorance, I looked around his room as I slowly undressed. Finally, once again, we could be alone together, with a closed door and quiet. But my stomach knotted. What would we do? What could we do? What did he want, desire? What were his limitations?

The amusing humming from the bathroom assured me that Everett was doing fine. Stripped down to my shorts, I nosed around at some of his books, a pile of cards from his schoolmates at Pinecrest Academy, handbooks and how-to guides for the newly handicapped. Next to them, a large shoebox tempted me. Knowing I shouldn't snoop, nonetheless I did.

Inside, a loose stack of all the letters I'd sent him lay nestled next to a cluster of dried wildflowers and pinecones.

As I fought back a shudder of emotion, I heard the toilet flush. Then, "Reid?"

Replacing the box lid, I stepped to the bathroom and ducked under the pull-up bars.

Under the shower, a built-in plastic seat with metal bars was Everett's intended goal. Beside the toilet, a plastic bag and tube lay empty.

"Okay, this is where you can help me," he said, reaching for his sweatpants with some difficulty as they tangled at his knees. I helped him finish, ducked back outside the bathroom to drop the sweats into the laundry basket. With a strange combination of awkward bashfulness and desire, I peeled off my shorts and socks, and stood naked in the doorway.

I fought back tears, pressing my lips together tightly, as if some stupid comment might burst out of me, some bleat of lust, pity or shame.

Everett had turned away to adjust the water temperature, and made a comedic double-take at the sight of me. "Wow."

"Wow to you, too."

"Are you okay?"

"Sure."

"Were you crying?"

"No. Yes. I'm just ... just happy to be with you."

Sitting there in that little tiled room, the hiss of the water, him naked, his arms flexed, about to rise, he stopped, looking me up and down.

He extended an arm.

"So, pick me up and put me on the seat."

As we touched, arms and shoulders and water spray and some awkward combination of him toying with my obvious desire, he said, "Somebody's happy to see me." The tenderness of scrubbing him, attending to him, brought up a wave of new feelings.

"I've never given anyone a bath," I confessed.

"Not even a dog?"

"Mom has allergies."

"Too bad." And then, as the water and suds made him squint, "Woof."

While his legs had thinned a bit, his arms and chest had thickened with muscle. Not only were we making up for lost time, but the combination of intimacy and water in yet another new location made lathering soap along his legs, waist and under his arms almost ecstatic for me. We were touching beyond the abrupt sexual urge; caressing, adoring, rediscovering.

Where was the therapy group for this? Among the many brochures in the lobby and on his desk, I hadn't noticed any that read, *How to Have Gay Sex With the Disabled.*

"Check this out," Everett turned to remove the low-placed showerhead from a clip-like holder. He gave himself a more thorough rinse before turning it on me. Startled, I jumped back against the tile wall as he hosed me down. I feigned annoyance as he aimed the spray lower. Wiping my eyes, I stood before him, growing harder where it counted, and relaxed everywhere else.

Everett set the showerhead down, turned to shut off the water, and sat before me, glistening wet, his dick pointing up between his legs. I felt a bit ashamed to feel relief at the sight of his excitement. So, he could do that. What would I have done if he couldn't?

Noticing my glance, he said, "Yeah, it works, sort of. It doesn't always…"

I waited.

"Here." He tossed a bar of soap at me, which I caught, sparing us any corny drop-the-soap jokes.

"Could you …?"

"Anything."

"Just ... jack off. Lemme just see you, your..."

I obeyed happily, awkwardly, then intensely, performing for him, my smiling little wet man.

As I got closer to coming, he gestured me closer, until he grasped it, tugged it, then with a growing ferocity, yanked an ejaculation out of me, aiming it onto himself. My legs quivered, buckled. I almost collapsed onto him, relieved that these new variations helped us avoid discussion and clarifications. So much pent up desire had compelled us through these new sensations and positions.

My playful reach for his cock, which had settled down a bit, was politely rebuffed. I figured it was time for us to rinse off again, to wipe him off and help him into his chair with a towel set on the seat. As I hovered near, he deigned a few kisses to parts of my arm and stomach.

Helping him slip on a pair of boxer shorts and a worn T-shirt, he then showed me how he got himself into the low bed, hopping over with minor difficulty, followed by the command, "Come 'ere. Kissin' time."

"Okay!"

"Wait." He requested a breath mint. "Over on the desk. Oh, and water."

I scanned the room.

"Mini-fridge."

I retrieved a bottle, found a cup.

"Bottle's fine."

I brought it, watched him drink. He offered, and I too drank.

"Okay, champ. Cozy up to your b-ball loser and gimme some sympathy."

I pressed myself against him. "I'm still not sure what..."

Not what, I wondered, but how. I knew his legs couldn't move, but his cock had sprouted up again, tenting his shorts, as if it knew what it wanted. I eased myself toward it, grasping his hand, preventing him from stopping me as I tugged his shorts down below his waist.

"It's okay," I soothed. "Just relax," I said to myself as much as to him.

He pulled off his shirt and asked me to shift the opposite way so we could do the same to each other. Everett wasn't entirely comfortable, but very determined. We readjusted ourselves a few times until we found a side-to-side position where his leg didn't fall onto my head.

Although I knew he couldn't feel my licks and tugs, his body responded. He clutched my hips with more force, signaling that he wanted me deeper in him. I had to look over to see his face, his eyes closed, his lips surrounding me. Before long he was soothingly swallowing my bursts with low appreciative hums.

"You couldn't wait for me again?" he joked, wiping his mouth.

"Sorry," I apologized. I grabbed his towel, wiped him off, then flipped around to nestle beside him. His cock had dwindled, but as I attempted to revive it, he took my hand away, brought it up to his stomach. I rubbed, soothed, caressed up around his chest, his neck, and we shared a few light kisses before he nestled close, my arm under his neck.

I continued touching him under his shorts and along his legs, determined to explore his thighs and hips, silently asking with my hands where his sensations began and ended.

"Could you rub my back a little? It's really tight."

"Anything you want," I smiled. Gently helping him roll over onto his stomach, I slowly caressed his back. My fingers found it before I saw it, the surgery scar above his butt. I turned my attention away, delicately straddled him, keeping my weight on my knees, and gave him a slow massage, guiding the tension out as he purred into the pillow.

Lowering myself atop him, my lingering erection nestled at the top cleft of his buttocks, pressing against his scar. We lay for a while, until he adjusted himself, signaling a desire to shift positions and roll onto his back.

Like a sort of erratic thermometer, his penis had thickened again, and I moved my face closer. I licked it, lubricating it, delicately tugging.

"Do you think you can …?"

"Let's find out."

As he laid back, his hand lightly rubbing my head and neck, I persisted, until his hips and legs began to spasm in a different and odd way. I didn't stop, until quite suddenly his dick erupted with a series of pent up volleys that splashed onto my face and hands.

"Oh, god. Oh, jeez, oh, fuck."

"Are you okay?" I almost panicked.

"Yeah, just … hold still."

I waited, impulsively licked up a few puddles, then adjusted back toward him and lay my head on his chest until his panting slowed.

"Whew!"

As the spasms diminished, I wiped my face and turned to look up to him. He lifted his head to grin at me.

Everett asked for the towel, which I retrieved, wiping myself off first. Before I returned to the bed, he held up his hand. "Wait. Just stand there."

"What?" I stood, naked and barefoot on the cool linoleum floor, and held out my arms. "Ta da."

"You're so tanned and, I dunno, more solid."

"Dorm food. I haven't run much in months, gained some weight."

"My woodland stud."

I returned to the bed, wiping him down, helping him tug his shorts back on before settling next to him, when he joked, "Now that was physical therapy I could get used to."

I grazed my hand along his cheek. "Your beard …"

"You like it?"

"Yeah, a lot."

I nuzzled closely to him, chafing my face on purpose.

"How long has it been?" I asked as he wiped a dribble from my neck.

"Well, how long's it been for you?"

"Um, other than humping a few trees, and Kevin, no one since you."

"Well, me too. Without Kevin, or trees."

We lay together for a while, until I ventured to ask, "What's it like?"

"What?" he asked.

"Coming. I mean, after ... now."

"That's funny should you ask, 'cause Daya gave me this whole embarrassing talk, part of my 'sexual counseling,' about how now that I've got some feeling back down there, it's almost important for me to get my rocks off. Greg gave me some pointers. He's pretty cool, for a straight guy."

"Oh, great. Is this going into your medical file?"

"Probably. Sorry, but your name did come up, since you're..."

"Your biped?"

He playfully elbowed me. "Anyway, speaking of coming, since you asked. It's like ... it starts inside me, and tingles in my bones and arms, like it spreads everywhere else. I can feel my dick, sort if, but like inside only, like pissing after a few beers used to feel. It's ... it's just different."

"It's good?"

"It's what it is. Come 'ere." We kissed again.

"Do you even jack off?" I asked as I grazed my fingers over his beard.

"I tried. It's weird, like I'm yanking some other guy's dick."

I wanted to half-joke that it sounded hot, but he seemed put off by the idea. "But you don't mind if I–"

"Oh, no. Have at it. But we have to be careful with, you know, the butt sex, 'cause I can't feel it, and you could tear my skin, and I'd get infected. You can poke around with your finger, which is what I have to do for, you know, 'elimination.'"

"Pinchin' a loaf?" I joked.

"Seein' a man about a horse."

We shared a few other terms amid chuckles.

"I'm also supposed to stimulate my prostate."

"Oh. I can help with that."

"But not like, with your big …"

"Got it."

"..hard…"

"That's okay. It's not my favorite thing."

He grinned, reached downward to rub my thigh. "And what is your favorite thing?"

I hesitated, considered the varied settings of our prior intimacy. I wanted to say, 'when that leaf landed on your back in the woods,' or 'the taste of your lips after drinking champagne,' or 'the glow of your skin with snow light reflecting on it.' Instead, I hinted, "That thing you did with your tongue."

"What thing?"

"You know, on New Year's Eve, with my butt."

He pretended to be perplexed.

"Analingus?"

Everett snorted out a laugh.

"What?" I cried, embarrassed. "You did it!"

"No, no, it's just …" He wrapped me in a hug, then reached down to flop his leg over mine. "We are gonna be so great together."

We lay together for a while, until he asked me to retrieve his catheter, "otherwise I'll pee all over you like a puppy."

I chuckled, then he did the same when my growling stomach sounded off.

"Hey, weren't we supposed to go to dinner?"

Arching his head up to check his alarm clock, Everett said, "Too late. Cafeteria's closed. I have some turkey and bread and stuff in the mini-fridge."

I got up and retrieved his catheter, then prepared some food, while still naked, at his command, and served it on his bed with exaggerated flair. He scooted himself up to sitting and we inhaled the sandwiches.

With the plates set aside, we nuzzled and dozed until well after dark. I mentioned a need to return to Holly's apartment, but Everett assured me that I could stay. He suggested I give his sister a call, which I did. She understood.

Beside him, his back to me after I'd returned to his bed and we'd shifted positions, I slipped one arm under his pillow as I nestled close behind him, my other hand free to graze his skin as his back rose and fell with slowing breaths. My silent tears of joy and relief lost in his still damp hair, I realized I didn't need that brochure.

Chapter 33

Even though Sundays were considered his day off from physical therapy, there were recreational days where Everett was supposed to work out unsupervised. I didn't know that would involve watching him face-dive from his braked chair over the edge of the pool.

Submerged below and rising near me, I felt a pang of fear for Everett's safety. But then I saw his water-blurred arm grab for me, and almost successfully yank my swimsuit down. I ducked back down toward him, and we playfully jostled underwater, until we both rose, gasped, shook the water from our eyes, and held on to each other, floating, grinning and giggling like little kids.

On the other side of the pool, a few senior patients, one in a funny flowered plastic bathing cap, were going through the motions of arm and leg exercises with their physical therapists. One of the younger quadriplegic kids was busily paddling around another adult. Anyone glancing at us would have thought I was simply helping Everett with some therapy. I guess I was.

The weight of his legs forced him to paddle harder, but he didn't seem to mind. Beneath the water, I saw the blurry image of his limbs, bent in a bobbing seated position. I held him at his waist, our faces inches apart. We performed an intimate aquatic pas de deux, everything beyond us whirling slowly in a blur.

"We should sneak in here at night sometime," I suggested.

"You learn from the master," Everett grinned. "But first, I'm hungry."

Everett swam toward the pool's edge. I was about to ask if he needed any help, but he hiked himself up to sitting with a wet plop. I followed, parked myself beside him, and realized that it was one of those rare new positions, other than in bed, where we were facing each other at the same level. I wanted to tell him how overwhelmed I was to simply have that moment with him, to just be a pair of guys sitting by a pool, our feet dangling in the water, to just be there, to just be.

Instead, I simply said, "Hi."

"Hi."

After changing back in his room, I followed his roll to the elevator and to the cafeteria, where he waved, low-fived or nodded at nearly all the other patients. Understandably, he'd yet again become a popular friend to many. We chose some of the above-average cafeteria food. Everett managed to hold a tray in his lap with ease.

"I was thinking," he said as we finally sat opposite each other at a table, "about sex."

"Better be careful with that."

"Well, I have been trying to meet new people."

"How's that going?"

"Greg's the only hot prospect, but he keeps bragging about his cunnilingus skills."

"Gross."

"Oh, you'll learn to appreciate his tips."

I snorted a laugh.

"So, how are things in 'Fill-dowf-ya?'"

More funny accent barbs. I smirked. "Groovy."

"Getting any?"

"Nope."

"Been saving yourself for me."

"Yup."

"That's it? You told me you're taking a PE course. Come on."

He had me. I quietly admitted to a few of my near encounters. He grinned, amused by my lurid tales, until I veered off course, saying, "but none of them were you."

He smiled, almost proud. "So, I told you I graduated from Pinecrest, finally."

"By mail."

"Yeah, they were pretty cool, considering they had to pay the insurance settlement. Well, their insurance company paid."

"So, are you thinking about college?" I asked.

"You know, my parents want me to go to Carnegie Mellon."

"And?"

"Reid, my boy," he said, cocking his head just so, "when have I ever listened to my parents?"

I smiled, refraining from mentioning my talk with Holly.

"But I'm still gonna move in with Dad, and maybe his new girlfriend, if he ever marries her, which may not happen. His condo's got a great view, doncha think?"

"Yeah, it does."

"So, you were saying, about Temple. There's a handicap dorm?"

"Yup," I said.

"And you said you already met a few wheelies?"

"But you'd probably be the only gay one."

"With a horny boyfriend eagerly awaiting my arrival."

"Yup."

"You're never gonna give up on me, are you?"

"Nope."

"Good."

I must have had the dopiest grin on my face. Everett reached across the table in what I thought would be a gesture of affection. Instead, he aimed his fork at my dessert.

"You gonna finish that?"

"I'm just getting started."

As we ate, I glanced around the cafeteria to other patients, most of them sitting with physical therapists in hospital blouses. One nearby young man around our age struggled to feed himself, his arms in a tangled knot. Everett waved, and the boy spilled a spoonful of food as he waved back, then shrugged as his attendant helped him clean up.

"Matthew; drunk driver victim. Sixteen. He'd just gotten his driver's license."

"Damn."

"We'll go hang out after lunch with him, if that's cool."

"Sure."

"He can't really talk very well."

"Oh. Um..."

"You're not freaked out or anything."

I couldn't say that a few truly troubled patients didn't make me want to turn away, or at least not stare.

"You know," Everett said, pushing his tray aside, "a few of my classmates came to visit, in the hospital, and here."

"That's nice."

"Yeah, but it was like ..." His turned his gaze away, focusing on some memory. "They all visited like they were supposed to, once. Some of them, they couldn't even look at me for long. They didn't really talk to me. They... talked around me." He returned to look at me, really see me. "Besides my family, you were the only one who kept coming back."

"That's their problem, not yours."

"That time, when I was upset–"

"Ev, you don't have to–"

"No, I do. You–"

And then it was his turn to choke up.

"The reason I ...asked you back to visit... I had some really long talks with Greg, and he basically bitch-slapped some sense into me. He made me realize some things, about us. I think I sent you away because I thought I was holding you back. I didn't want you to have to deal with all this while I'm still trying to do it myself."

"Right."

"But thinking about you made me want to keep going, stop whining, after that. I missed you so much. I just wanted to wait until I was okay with me."

"Thanks, Monkey."

"So, are we okay?"

He knew I'd wait. He was everything to me. "After last night," I blushed. "I think we're more than okay."

Everett smirked. "Why? Because I shot a big load?"

"What? No!"

"No, really. I'm happy that I can, you know, function. But that's not gonna happen much."

"I know. Well, I didn't know, but that's not... Ev, please."

"What?"

"It's not about that."

"I know."

"I mean, it's not just about that."

We smiled, held hands across the table, then toyed with the remains of our lunch, until Everett remarked, "That was a geyser, though, wasn't it? Damn!"

His volcanic self-impersonation left me stifling laughter until pretty much everyone in the cafeteria was staring at us.

Chapter 34

Along with the overwhelming first semester of class homework, another thing I learned at Temple was that every request had a form. Changing dormitories had a form, as did getting permission to move my spartan belongings in boxes from one room to another before the winter break. Hauling my stuff across the state twice would be a waste of time, so I persisted, trekking from one administrative office to another, keeping multiple colored, signed and stamped forms for those forms.

Despite there being a few vacancies among the dual resident handicapped dorm rooms, housing an able-bodied student who wasn't "an assigned caregiver" was noted by a suspicious clerk as an "irregularity" that required even more forms.

Devon had been helpful with hints about who to talk to at the various offices. As I had scrawled notes and taken down names, he'd also mentioned how difficult winters would be on campus. "They plow the snow on the street, but forget to get the curbs," he'd said. "It's a bitch getting' around sometimes." On the side of the list of things I'd need for the next semester, I'd written, 'Snow Shovel.'

"What's all that?" Eric asked after I'd returned to our dorm room and plopped a fresh pile of paperwork onto my desk.

"My friend's enrolling here next semester," I said, gesturing toward my desk with a smile. Shortly after my visit with Everett, I'd bought some small cheap frames at the student bookstore and placed a few of Holly's photos on my desk; the innocuous one of us sitting in her apartment, and another of Everett on the basketball court. Any explanation of our intimacy was upstaged by Eric's fascination with the pure biomechanics of life with a wheelchair.

Eric had been surprisingly sympathetic when I had revealed the purpose of my move. It was only weeks before the semester's end that I'd waited to explain to him that Everett was more than a close friend. He wasn't surprised.

He even helped me pack and haul boxes across campus, during which he occasionally asked questions that had never come up, mostly to do with my being gay, Everett's accident, and the intersection of the two. It was a bit awkward, but I had begun to learn how to be honest and not so secretive, since his curiosity seemed sincere.

The informal party held in our common room the night of our last day of classes promised a bit of the beer-induced rowdiness that had spread across the university. Outside our window, streams of toilet paper fluttered in the breeze from a few trees. Random hoots and hollers echoed down the hallways. Parking lots and driveways had become clustered with cars being loaded with luggage and boxes by students eager to leave.

The jovial atmosphere in our dorm, aided by a few other guys from nearby rooms who heard there was beer, almost came to an abrupt halt when my only guest appeared at the open door.

"Hey, glad you could make it!" I stood and greeted Devon, who rolled in cautiously.

There was the slightest pause in the party as everyone's attention shifted to his entrance. I hadn't told any of them that I'd invited him. In fact, I had secretly decided to use the occasion to test them and see how nonchalant they could be.

After some awkward introductions, as I'd anticipated, the entire conversation began to focus on Devon, who had to answer a series of innocuous and uninformed questions about his life, in particular, what he could and could not do. The semi-drunken queries turned to the expected topic.

"How do you have sex?" Charlie, one of my soon-to-be-former roommates blurted.

"How do you?" Devon smiled.

"With a pillow," his roommate Dennis joked. Charlie blushed and slinked off to get more beer.

"Guys, come on," I said.

"It's cool," Devon assured me before replying to the others. "Actually, I get hit on by girls a lot. But you know, it's more about pleasing them." He made an amusingly crude mimed gesture of parting a pair of legs with his hands and licking. "And they get that." He grinned.

"What, they ride your chair?" another guy asked.

"Sometimes."

Satisfied with his boasts, the guys finally warmed up to Devon. Eric tossed out a volley of questions more to do with biomechanics and technology, most of which left Devon befuddled.

I pulled a chair close to him, dismissing the meandering conversation of the others, which descended to more base sexual topics.

"Is it always like that?" I asked.

"What?"

"People asking you stupid questions."

"Depends on who I hang with. Isn't it like that with your friend?"

"I don't know." I considered how my bond with Everett would be tested. We had never been with people who weren't either his or my family or other disabled people and staff at the rehab center. Outside the campus, the city had at first been bewildering to me. While I found myself taking mental notes at the sight of each ramped curb, I wondered if Everett would find it overwhelming.

I considered the divide I would have to balance in public. Would my protective nature prove too defensive? I had felt a sliver of panic in the new dorm room, empty except for my boxes and duffle bags of clothes. Peering at the handicap-accessible fixtures, I wondered if I understood all of the responsibilities.

Living with Everett would be a dream fulfilled. I hoped the pangs of longing would settle to a daily pleasure, a normalcy. But the ignorant remarks, the possible insults and curiosity of others – how would that fit into our new life?

Actually, I was afraid. Being together every day would change everything. Despite what had happened to him, or partly because of it, I expected Everett would draw admirers of all kinds. Would I become jealous? Too protective? Too possessive?

Unsure how to share all this with Devon, I simply said, "Everett can handle himself."

I hoped I was right.

Chapter 35
Winter, 1980

As much as my parents at first dreaded the idea of spending a New Year's Day lunch at the home of the Forresters, at least it offered an excuse to shorten our traditional family visit to Scranton. For that, my mother was thrilled.

That morning, I'd taken a walk before either of them had awakened. When I returned, the smell of brewing coffee filled the kitchen.

"Where've you been?"

"Secret mission."

Mom didn't request an explanation.

After our breakfast at home, where we each withheld our different kinds of apprehension, we changed into dressy holiday-colored clothes. My father put on a tie and jacket. I donned a dark green sweater, which I wore only at Christmas, since it itched.

My mother's outfit was quite impressive. She kept Dad and I waiting, but with her hair and make-up complete, a traditional skirt and blouse of green and red, she was stunning. Perhaps Dad didn't see how expertly she managed to resemble one of those old magazine ad housewives. To her, it was all a fun joke.

The short drive was filled with mild jests about curtailing our sarcastic comments or remarks about the visible wealth of our hosts.

"Their house isn't *that* big," I lied.

"As long as they don't start talking politics," Dad sighed. He and my mother had been more than disappointed by Ronald Reagan's election.

My dad parked in the driveway behind Holly's car. Next to it was a blue Chevy van. I wasn't sure who else had been invited, but it didn't look like it belonged to anyone I knew.

Diana Forrester welcomed us at the door with a combination of falsified affection and graceful formality.

Everett sat in his chair by the fireplace, as comfortably as anyone else, a satisfied grin on his face. After a round of greetings, hugs and handshakes, I ended up parking myself at the only free spot, on the end of a sofa at the opposite end of the room.

Visibly miffed at the arrangement, in the middle of his mother's request for a toast, and a pronouncement about this possibly being their last Christmas together before selling their house, Everett upstaged her and scooted himself across the room to be beside me.

Over eggnog and coffee, tree cookies and pie on tiny plates set upon laps, the conversation flitted like a butterfly over the truth, but I didn't mind. Diana and Carl expertly imitated affection and remained cordial.

Everett and I stole flirtatious glances, quietly satisfied. The guise that he and I were merely roommates-to-be held ground, despite everyone's knowledge.

Diana Forrester refused to openly admit the truth, and that was just fine. The gathering had been requested –probably demanded– by Everett, but his mother made it seem as though it was all her doing.

The night before, I'd been allowed to accompany Everett at Mrs. Forrester's New Year's Eve party as a second pseudo-servant/guest, with the assurance that we keep our displays of affection at least behind closed doors. She wouldn't know that he and I had reached a calming balance, that merely being together, and knowing that we would soon be together almost every day, was enough, *pro tempore.*

By New Year's Day, a sort of truce had been established between his mother and me, I realized. Mrs. Forrester refused to consent to my victory, that I had taken him away from her, in a way. She kept her head held high, acknowledged Everett's tremendous progress, not thanking me, just sharing her pride in her son.

"It just makes more sense for us, for Everett, to have more functional homes for him to visit," Mrs. Forrester said. "The estimates we got for stair ramps and converting bathrooms was just astronomical."

Holly kept her eye-rolling disdain to a minimum, and took a few informal photos of us, calmly, so she could get the warm lighting of the room without using a flash.

Being of legal age, we each indulged in the mildly spiked eggnog until our shared burps brought giggles from Holly.

"Didja see the wheels?" he said.

"You got a new chair?"

"No, brainiac; the van."

"Oh, yeah. Whose is that?"

"Now that I got my driver's license, mine."

"What?"

"You've heard about Everett's little present, I take it." Everett's father had sidled up beside us. "His friend Kevin told me his father was looking to sell a used van with handicap adjustments. They gave us quite a deal; practically gave it to us."

"Wow. So, you can drive it?"

Everett beamed with pride. "Who do you think's taking us to Philly next week?"

"Damn. And all I got you was a sled."

Everett laughed it off, but actually, I felt rather trumped. His gift to me, while impractical, was charmingly sentimental; a small stuffed toy giraffe.

Before returning to the adults, Mr. Forrester said, "Be sure to thank your friend Kevin before you leave for school."

"We will," Everett smiled, before quietly nudging me, "You already did, once."

I held up three fingers.

Everett's burst of shocked laughter caused his mother to suggest that we retreat to the den. Holly followed us. Between the piano, a card table, and board games and books stacked on a shelf, we entertained ourselves.

Plopping herself down on a sofa, Holly said, "What she really doesn't want is her son scuffing her precious wooden floors and carpeting with his dirty wheels."

Everett spun himself around in a half-wheelie, deliberately twisting the carpet into a wrinkled hump. Holly gasped.

He settled back on his wheels, grinning like a cat. "She wanted me to pose for our annual stiff holiday portrait sitting on the sofa, without my chair," he grumbled, shaking his head in disbelief.

Disturbed by his palpable if not understandable parental disdain, I abruptly changed the subject and asked to take a few pictures with Holly's camera of the two of them together. We gossiped and shared highlights from our few months of conspiratorial misadventures.

"Hey, take me upstairs to my old room," Everett said, bored or anxious. "I have some stuff for you. I'll show you the van later when we load it up."

I consented, wondering if we could get away with our recently discovered off-chair travel mode in the house.

One of our few private days together over the holidays included an afternoon drive to Twin Lakes Park. After telling him of my childhood memories of the park, at Everett's request, I had even brought my ranger hat.

After finding a nestled private glen, we had parked his chair along the path. The trail was short enough for me to let him ride on my back for a brief walk. We'd cuddled together in the cold for a while, sipped cocoa from a Thermos Helen insisted on giving us.

Bringing that intimate piggyback walk's method out in the open, among family and in his home, made me hesitate.

"Come on, stud," Everett commanded. "Back it up."

"Wait. Where's Mister Pee-buddy?"

"What's Mister Peabody?" Holly asked.

"Inside joke," Everett said. We'd since made up a slew of silly terms for his catheter and disposable underpants. "Don't worry," he said, waving me toward him. "It's a 'granny pants' day."

"Okay, then." Aiming my rear end toward Everett's lap, I crouched down as he wrapped his arms around my neck. A few scoots of shifting his chest higher up my back accomplished, we stood up. I grabbed behind myself to hoist his legs.

Mrs. Forrester spotted us in the hallway and shouted, "Be careful!"

Everett muttered into my ear, "Like I'll get crippled again?"

Holly hauled Everett's wheelchair up the stairs as I followed, Everett muttering, "hup, hup, hup" into my ear with each step, encouraging me to jog harder.

Once eased into his chair at the top of the stairs, Holly left for her bedroom, and Everett rolled away to dig around in his bedroom closet. "It's mostly just my dirty old sneakers. Oh, wait."

"Old jock straps?"

"Better." Beaming with pride, he extracted a Rock 'Em Sock 'Em Robots toy set. Piling up old sports equipment and toys, I marveled at his odd gesture. He didn't need to pack for days.

A thrilled gasp down the hall grabbed Everett's attention. He wheeled off to Holly's room as she sifted through her own childhood possessions. I found myself dutifully packing boxes with their trusty housekeeper, who'd followed us upstairs. As always, Helen was determined to supervise.

A burst of adult laughter from downstairs, the loudest of which was my father's, assured me that things were going fine below. I helped Helen put some of

Everett's things in boxes for his move to college; clothes he liked and could change into and out of more easily, a few framed pictures, and his mother's Cole Porter records.

Helen asked how he was doing. I told her of his exercise regimen, the university campus, and his scruffy beard, which he'd shaved before returning home for the holidays.

"How about you?"

"Me?"

"Yes, you," she said.

I explained how I had met with my college advisor. My partial scholarship would remain, even though I'd already decided on a shift in my major. I'd added a physical therapy class, and even an architecture class.

"You're going to design buildings?"

"Ramps, for public parks."

"He's changed all our lives so much," she said.

"For the better, right?"

Actually, Everett's fate would lead to Helen eventually losing her job. Yet she said, "I think so."

"I know so," I smiled, clueless as well.

"Are you happy?"

"Every time I think of him."

Helen folded a sweater and said, "I guess people who are meant to be together will always find their way."

"Yes, Ma'am."

After the family lunch, I bid my parents farewell as they drove off in their car. I then shuttled Everett out the door in his chair, which we left on the porch after I'd helped him into the red plastic sled.

Tugging him across the street with the sled's plastic cord, Everett sang a haphazard and somewhat bawdy medley of holiday songs as I led him down the path, across the partially frozen stream and up the snow-covered ivy bank, over to the hillside, and under that strip of evergreen trees, where we celebrated our anniversary in our own way.

Stopping the sled under that awning of branches, each of us stuffed into parkas, gloves and boots, Everett laughed when he saw it.

"Bring me closer." I gave the sled another tug.

Nestled just under the much taller trees, but close enough to the clearing to get enough sunlight, the little tree he'd given back to me sprouted up through the layer of snow. That morning, my 'secret mission' accomplished, its tiny branches held a few small red and gold ornaments.

"That is so perfect, so Charlie Brown," he said, touching it lightly.

"Actually, Linus was the one who did that."

"Smart ass."

I took a blanket from Everett's lap, set it beside him on the snow, and sat facing him.

"It's grown."

"About a foot," I added.

"Sweet."

We both admired it for a while, until he looked at me, beaming, his cheeks already flushed from the cold.

"So, roomie," he grinned.

"Yeah, roomie?"

"I have to warn you, I come from an underprivileged background."

"Oh, really?" I asked.

"Yes, I've never learned the skill of personal housekeeping, so I shall require assistance."

"In learning how to do it your own damn self?"

He chuckled. "Actually, I'm a total clean freak. They forced it on us at school."

"Only one alpha male per room, huh?"

"Yes, and that would be me."

"We'll see about that."

He reached for me with a playful swat, missed. I scooted closer, the sled dividing us. An accidental glove full of snow brushed our faces as we hugged. I pulled him back to see his face, glistening with melting snow.

We kissed. He nudged forward, then shoved, intentionally bringing us rolling over onto the ground, until he lay atop me.

Gasping and laughing, shaking off clumps of snow, I began to babble on about all the terrific plans I had for us; the distance from our dorm to the pool, a flat trail he could roll on as I ran, even the wheelchair basketball league he could join.

But then I stopped. All I could hear was my own voice, until it didn't make any sense. Sighing, my breath steamed up toward him. I saw that with his look, this boy, who for so long had me dazzled beyond sense, was now awestruck by me.

"What?"

He hovered over me. "You are so amazing. You're really ready for this."

"For what?"

"You know; the big city, moving, cohabitation..."

"Shackin' up."

"That sounds much better."

I recalled that moment of anxious anticipation I'd felt in the empty dorm room. But it was too late to be afraid.

As if sensing my thoughts, he said, "You know it's not gonna be easy."

"When has being with you ever been easy?"

With his gloved hands on the ground at either side of me, he arched up, looked around, not with caution, but to survey our domain, then back down to me, pressing light kisses on my face, kisses that became more intense as our lips met.

Between the rustle of our parkas and a few giggles and grunts, the blanketed silence of the snowy woods surrounded us. The branches above swayed slowly, intertwined.

EVERY TIME I THINK OF YOU

ABOUT THE AUTHOR

Jim Provenzano is the author of the novels *PINS, Monkey Suits, Cyclizen*, the Lambda Literary Award-nominated *Every Time I Think of You*, the stage adaptation of *PINS*, as well as numerous published short stories and freelance articles. The curator of *Sporting Life*, the world's first LGBT athletics exhibit, he also wrote the syndicated 'Sports Complex' column for ten years. An editor with the *Bay Area Reporter*, he lives in San Francisco. www.jimprovenzano.blogspot.com

Made in the USA
Charleston, SC
08 August 2012